THE C

The norm
covered in slime. The woods were
carpeted in the rarest of wild flowers.
For Ben and Julia an ordinary summer holiday is turned into the most
spectacular adventure. Is the mysterious arrival of Hal, so foreign and
yet so familiar, the key to it all? The
key to the future?

THE
CUCKOO
PLANT

ADAM FORD

TEENS · MANDARIN

First published in Great Britain 1991 by Teens
an imprint of Mandarin Paperbacks
Michelin House, 81 Fulham Road, London SW3 6RB

Mandarin is an imprint of the Octopus Publishing Group

ISBN 0 7497 0613 9

A CIP catalogue record for this title
is available from the British Library

Printed in Great Britain
by Cox & Wyman Ltd, Reading, Berkshire

CONTENTS

CHAPTER 1

Opal Moon

'Hey, look!'

There was no need to point. All the faces at the bus stop were faintly illuminated as simultaneously they turned to stare at the sky.

'What is it?'

'A shooting star?'

'A satellite?'

Several heads shook in wonder.

'More like a rocket burning up.'

'Or a comet?'

'No way . . . comets don't cross the sky that fast.'

'I think its a UFO . . . a flying saucer,' a woman said in a hushed whisper.

'It's flying from west to east,' an authoritative voice stated firmly. 'So it's probably a satellite disintegrating on re-entry.'

A blazing blue fireball was climbing from the horizon to the zenith of the sky. It grew even brighter as it passed high overhead.

'Oh!'

Every one gasped as the fireball suddenly flared, trailing a stream of fire behind it.

'It's like bonfire night,' someone giggled.

The normal silence of the bus queue had been broken.

'It can't be a shooting star,' said Ben, 'it's lasting too long . . . they're usually gone in a second or two.'

'Unless it's a meteorite – I wonder where it will land?'

'North Sea?'

'Russia?'

The fireball was brighter now than a full moon. The small crowd edged a few paces up the pavement to keep it in view as it fell down the sky beyond a building. The whole landscape from the edge of town right out to the woods on the distant line of hills was bathed in an eerie blue light. The stars disappeared in the glow of the false dawn. It was like a fake stage-set for a film of an alien world. Moments later the fireball sank beneath the eastern horizon, setting beyond the range of hills. A deeper darkness set over the badly-lit street. Everyone was silent until a woman's voice broke in.

'I still think it was a UFO.'

'Or a secret missile . . . a bit of star war stuff,' someone suggested.

'Not so secret!' Someone else laughed.

The bus suddenly drew up.

'Nuclear waste,' announced the bus driver

8

to each passenger as they fumbled for change and slowly climbed aboard. 'It's those cost-cutting politicians who are to blame. That stuff was supposed to go into high orbit and stay clear of Earth for ever. Now it's come back to pollute us.' No-one bothered to argue with him.

Julia and Ben had just put their change on the shelf by the driver, when they heard a car horn honking urgently. Ben grabbed their fares and they quickly jumped off the bus before its doors closed.

'Make up your bloomin' minds,' shouted the driver crossly. They ran twenty yards up the road and got into their father's car.

'Sorry I nearly missed you,' he said. 'I stopped to watch that thing in the sky. Wasn't it fantastic?' Noise from the car's engine and the subdued sound of music from the radio shut out the world outside. They missed the deep rumble that came from the sky a few minutes later. Shock waves from the fireball ran through the atmosphere. A roar like distant thunder rolled across the clear night sky.

'Every one at the bus stop thought it was a UFO,' Julia said leaning forward from the back seat to put her head between Ben and her father.

'Everyone?!' Ben mocked. 'You are a pratt . . . *one* woman said she thought it might be. I tell you . . . It was a fireball.'

'So what's a fireball when it's at home then?' Julia rejoined defensively, sitting well back in her seat.

'A fireball? Well it's a . . . a . . .' he began.

'Go on . . . you don't know. You're only saying it was a fireball because that man said so.'

'Now stop it, you two . . . you're always bickering. I can't think how you manage to stay together for an evening.'

'What do you think it was, Dad?' Julia asked trying to sidestep the argument. She was feeling a bit silly about her UFO remark.

Her father shrugged his shoulders.

'Shooting star . . . satellite burning up . . . I don't know. I just hope it doesn't crash down on anyone.'

The radio played pop music from a local station. Julia stared out of the window. Her face, darkly reflected in the glass, was superimposed on the black silhouette of hedgerows flying past. Her thick hair spread out wildly on each side of her face: her mother would almost certainly tell her to brush it. She dismissed the thought instantly and pressed her nose against the cold glass. This way she could just make out one or two of the brighter stars. Reflections of the light on the dashboard got confused with the sky so that it seemed as though some stars moved. The hedgerow ahead of them, lit up by the car headlights, formed a bright tunnel through the darkness. Overhanging trees increased the impression of being in an enclosed world.

This must be how it feels to be a rabbit in its burrow, she thought. Thinking of rabbits and burrows made her think of the field up behind their house. In only two days she would be the proud owner of a horse. Well, at least for a couple of months. A friend of her mother's had offered to lend it for the summer. A neighbouring farmer had said she could keep it in the field. She could ride every day for weeks and weeks as school holidays had been extended while the building was made safe. Everything was going her way! Julia stared out of the window with unseeing eyes, transported in daydream to the rides she would have.

'Sh! . . . Listen,' said Ben.

The music on the radio had faded; a voice had come on the air.

'Here is a news flash. Reports are coming in from all over the north of England of a dramatic fireball.'

Ben grinned. 'Fireball,' he whispered.

'. . . Eye witnesses from places as far apart as Newcastle and Chester are reporting a blazing blue unidentified flying object.' (It was Julia's turn to look smug for a moment.) 'The object, whatever it is, is now somewhere over Scandinavia. Keep tuned to this station . . . we'll keep you up to date with events.'

The pop music continued. They were nearly

home and just passing the cottage where their neighbour Mrs Birtwhistle lived.

'Mrs B.'s not in bed yet,' said Julia seeing the light.

'I don't think she goes off very early,' her father said, '. . . she was telling me she doesn't sleep much – not since her husband died a year ago. It must be lonely for her, poor thing.'

Within an hour of their arriving home, ITV had put together a full report on the fireball with telephoned interviews with astronomers. The object – still unidentified – had circled the planet. After streaking high in the stratosphere over the north of England it had crossed the North Sea, then Norway, and then it had flamed its way across the vast empty steppes of Russia. It crossed the Pacific in daylight like a bright star in the blue sky. In the USA people had followed its spectacular trajectory with binoculars and small telescopes. Finally, it faded and vanished over the eastern Atlantic just before its second flight across the British Isles.

Experts disagreed. It could have been a fireball, that is to say a bright meteorite, but the astronomer royal doubted it. Fireballs had never been known to circle the planet before. The military establishments of the nations so far contacted remained silent. Nobody claimed it as their satellite. This meant, some people concluded, that it was top secret and therefore the public would never know what it was. Clearly there was great concern in official circles – ships and aircraft along the western seaboard of Europe were put on alert and directed to search the ocean for debris.

Mrs Birtwhistle peered out into the shadows of the lane for her cat. She stood at the gate at the end of her garden path. Moonlight cast a stillness over everything. The road was quiet; not many vehicles came this way at this late hour.

'Puss, puss!' She paused and listened.

She called again. But she knew that if her cat had smelt a mouse it would be out hunting all night. She waited a little longer, then decided to give up. Turning to return to her cottage she looked up at the moon. She stopped.

The moon was changing colour. First red then green then violet. Then all the colours of the rainbow mixed and swirled as they do in a soap bubble.

'Oh my!' she whispered, transfixed.

She had heard tell of blue moons, but never multi-coloured ones. Her cat slid silently between the bars of the gate and started to rub against her leg. She bent down to stroke him; staring all the while up at the sky.

As she gazed she was transported for a moment back to childhood. Her grandmother used to have a very special box on her Victorian dressing-table. In it was a ring. An opal ring. The moon was her grandmother's opal ring.

As she watched, the colours faded away until the full moon shone with its usual bright yellow light. Now she could see that there was something up there in the sky, a sort of thin cloud, like a veil. As she watched, a shock like a fast ripple seemed to run through its length and breadth. The veil, which had drifted in such a leisurely way across the face of the moon, was now taking charge of its own flight. It pulled itself together, rolling up and furling neatly in a long tube. Turning at a sharp angle it pointed purposefully downward and with a flick it darted out of the sky like a silvery fish in the moonlight down towards the ground. She lost sight of it for a moment as it shot behind the trees. It must have levelled out because seconds later, it whistled with the sound of a flute across Mrs Birtwhistle's rooftop.

She ducked involuntarily and watched with astonishment as the object skimmed low over the fields beyond her house. It followed the upward slope of the land weaving its way expertly between the tall trees like a wingless ghost plane. Seconds later it headed straight for a dark patch of trees, known locally as Filkins Wood, and vanished.

The cat rubbed against her legs and clouds drifted across the moon.

CHAPTER 2

Pond Weed

A cuckoo, the first Julia had heard that spring, called from the direction of Filkins Wood. It was a clear call commanding attention. She climbed down off the stile and stood for a moment in the long grass that skirted the field. It was still wet with dew. It was a fresh morning and no one else was up yet. Julia had found it impossible to stay in bed once the sun was shining through her window. She had dressed quickly intending to rig up a couple of jumps in the field.

There it was again! This time the cuckoo called from further to the right, its flute-like notes carrying clearly across the countryside. It must be flying from tree to tree to mark out its territory, she thought. If she waited it might fly this way and land in one of the trees in the garden. She had never seen the cuckoo, although Ben and her elder brother John had seen it many times – or so they said. She waited, but it called again from the same place and then a minute or two later from further afield.

An old carthorse had grazed the field through some of the winter months. The grass was still short except around the perimeter in the ditch that flanked the hedge. Julia waded through the wet grass, searching for the old gate the farmer had said she could use as a jump, until her jeans were soaked from the knee down. She found two rusty oil drums and set them up on end. The field was reasonably flat here and covered in molehills.

Continuing to hunt for the gate, she made her way up the long hedge to the top corner of the field. A gap in the hedge between two ash trees, with their black buds waiting to burst, led out into the muddy lane which ran all the way down past her house in one direction and up the hill to the fields beneath Filkins Wood in the other.

At last she spied the discarded gate. At first sight the moss-covered wood looked rotten; it was wet and dark. But when she gave the gate a tug, it was solid and very heavy. She tried pulling again and it moved. She leaned backwards and tugged with all her might. With a jerk the old dead brambles released their grip and the gate swung over and down with a thud.

'Damn!' she cried in pain. The top of the gate had caught her shin as it fell. She hopped about furious with herself. The sharp stinging in her shin brought a prickle of tears to her eyes.

'Damn! Damn!' She stopped hopping and inspected her leg. It was grazed and red but there was no blood. Slowly the stinging subsided and she was able to cup her hand over the painful area.

The gate lay heavily where it had fallen, flattening the long grass beneath it. There was no way she would be able to drag the gate by herself to where she had set up the two oil drums. Ben would have to help her.

Suddenly, louder than she had ever heard it before, the cuckoo called just above her head. It was in the ash tree itself. Julia squinted up trying to see the bird, but the limbs of the tree were dark against the bright sky. A flock of small birds, chaffinches and hedgesparrows, were making a great commotion in the hedgerow.

Then she saw it. The cuckoo was on a low branch and had turned its head. Almost immediately, it took to the wing and passing no more than a couple of feet above her flew out and down across the field like a grey hawk hunting. The flock of small birds gave chase and mobbed the cuckoo all the way. At the bottom of the field it turned and skimmed along the hedge, finally disappearing amongst the trees at the back of her house.

Did the smaller birds know why they mobbed the cuckoo? she wondered. Or was it just blind habit? And if they mobbed it now so energetically, why did they obediently foster its offspring

later – and then have to pay for the privilege
with the ejection of their own children from
the nest?

The cuckoo called again and it seemed to her
that it must be perched in the very tree where
Ben had rigged up a swing. The pain in her leg
was forgotten; she felt hungry and ran home.

'I just don't know how we're going to get
through this extra holiday, Mrs B,' Dorothy
Garstang said in despair. 'It's such a nuisance
about the school closing. I do wish they would
think of parents – they only gave us two days'
notice.'

'They should have let you know at the beginning of the Easter holidays,' Mrs Birtwhistle
agreed. She had her hands in the kitchen sink
peeling potatoes. For years she had helped out
at the Garstangs' a couple of days a week –
particularly in the school holidays. They needed
the extra help – Dorothy Garstang had a job
in a solicitor's office in town, with reasonably
flexible hours. Dick, her husband, worked on
the management side of a construction company
and rarely got home before 7.00 o'clock in the
evening.

'You'd think it would be easier now John's at
university,' Dorothy Garstang continued. 'But
I don't think I dare leave the other two on
their own together. They quarrel and fight all
the time.'

'Don't you worry about them two. They'd be wet sops if they didn't argue a bit. And anyway, I bet that when you're not there they get on like a house on fire!' She looked out of the window to the top of the garden where Julia and Ben were deep in conversation. Ben was sitting on the ground while Julia swung slowly in the car tyre, which he had suspended from a branch of the largest apple tree.

'At least Julia's got a horse coming – that'll keep her occupied.' Dorothy Garstang tried to reassure herself. 'And last night I promised Ben I'd pay for him to have a course in windsurfing. That'll keep him out of Julia's way most mornings.'

'Just look!' Mrs B. pointed out of the kitchen window. 'Look how they talk . . . they're as thick as thieves. I don't know why you worry.'

'Probably hatching a plot,' sighed their mother.

'There you go!' beamed Mrs B. 'If they argue you think they are enemies . . . and if they get on then they're hatching a plot! You know what I think? . . . you worry too much. They'll come to no harm left to themselves for a day or two.'

There was a clatter at the back door. Ben burst into the kitchen followed by Julia.

'Can I have some breakfast, Mum?' demanded Ben.

'But I've put everything away . . . I thought you'd had breakfast already?'

'He did . . . hours ago with me,' interjected Julia. 'He just wants some more.'

'Shut up you!' Ben flung at her. 'I only had a bit of toast. And now I'm really hungry. After dragging that stupid gate right down the field I should think I deserve a breakfast.'

'It's not a stupid gate!'

'You should see the mad jump she's rigged up. Two oil drums and a rotten gate!'

'I don't want your opinion,' she countered, 'anyway that's just how they set up jumps at the riding stables.'

'Unsafe if you ask me.'

'Well, I'm not asking you.'

'It was your brawn she wanted, love, not your brains,' joked Mrs B., handing him a breakfast bowl from the shelf.

'All right,' his mother agreed, 'have some cereals if you want — but mind you clear up afterwards and wash your bowl. I don't want to find it tonight, when I come home, on the floor in front of the T.V. . . . like I did yesterday.'

'That was Julia . . . not me,' said Ben with indignation.

'Huh!' exploded Julia 'It was not me!'

'Now, you two,' interrupted Mrs B. 'I've just been telling your mother how well you get on . . . so don't let me down.'

'Get on?' Ben and Julia echoed, each pulling a face of disgust.

'Last night,' Mrs B. began with great emphasis changing the subject 'I saw the oddest thing'

'The fireball?'

'Wasn't it fantastic?'

'No – not that, though I did hear about that on the news this morning. What I saw was much odder.'

Julia and Ben glanced at each other and their eyes ever so briefly rolled up to the ceiling. Mrs B. was something of a gossip.

'Here we go,' whispered Julia as she leant across Ben to reach the milk for her coffee.

'I was calling my cat in from the lane . . . it was late . . . when I saw the moon. It was turning all colours. All reds and greens and blues . . . it put me in mind of my grandmother's opal ring.'

'Well I've heard of blue moons . . .' Dorothy Garstang interrupted doubtfully.

'That's exactly what I thought . . .' continued Mrs B. in full flow. 'But then would you believe it – something was floating in front of the moon. Flapping in the wind it was like a great sheet of flimsy washing. But then do you know what? As I watched it all rolled up – like a blind does. And it shot out of the sky, just like a jet plane. "Woosh" it went; straight between my chimney pots. It flew off real fast up towards Filkins Wood.'

'Extraordinary!' said Dorothy Garstang but then added cautiously, 'But are you sure?'

'I expect it was the drink!' Ben mumbled through a mouth full of cornflakes.

21

For a moment there was a shocked silence.

'Ben! How dare you speak to Mrs Birtwhistle like that. Apologise at once.'

Ben was flustered. He'd meant to be funny. He stood up and ran his fingers through his blond hair. He did this so often that his hair lay straight back now from his forehead.

'Sorry, Mrs B.' He looked straight at her and tried a smile. But the atmosphere had gone distinctly cool. Everyone knew that Mrs B. liked a drink of port in the evening. But she was a bit touchy about the subject.

'Whatever it was you saw,' insisted Ben's mother, 'I think you should tell the police. You never know what's going on in the skies these days. It may have been one of those experimental planes they fly out over the sea . . . or maybe a parachute . . . yes, I expect that was it . . . a parachute.' Secretly, she wondered whether old age and living on her own weren't making Mrs B. a bit dotty.

There was a bang from the back door. Ben followed by Julia had made a tactful escape into the garden.

'You are a clot!' said Julia. 'And you left your breakfast bowl again!'

'Oh, forget it,' shrugged Ben, 'Mrs B. will wash it up. Anyway . . . I'm not going back in there now.'

Ben kicked at an old football that lay in his

22

path. It rocketed into the shrubs at the top of the garden.

'I could have bitten my tongue off,' he admitted.

'But what an imagination!' Julia suddenly laughed. 'She does get carried away sometimes. I thought she was going to say that little green men had landed in her garden!'

Ben had climbed on to the tyre he had rigged up on a rope and was swinging with great determination.

'I know what we'll do!' he shouted, and leaping off the swing rolled over twice. He stood up and brushed the leaves off his clothes. 'We'll go up to Filkin's Wood. Then we can tell her that there's nothing there to worry about. Then she'll think that it was a joke about the drink . . . and that really I believed her.'

At the top of the field they turned into the muddy lane. Overgrown hawthorn and hazel bushes hung across the lane meeting overhead in many places. Large oak trees cast deeper shadows.

A quarter of a mile up the lane they turned right into a field of uncut hay. They skirted the field in order to avoid trampling the crop. The hedges were lower here; they had been cut back in the autumn. They stopped for a moment, and looked back the way they had come.

'The sea!' they chanted in unison.

'I saw it first!' The ritual of who saw it first went back further than either of them could remember. They surveyed the distant blue horizon.

'Tomorrow I'll be out there,' said Ben sweeping the skyline with a grand gesture,' flashing across the stormy waves on my windsurf board.'

'Stormy waves!' laughed Julia, 'There's not a white horse in sight! Anyway you'll fall in!' She gave him a shove.

'Look,' he pointed, ignoring her last remark, 'you can see windsurfers out there now.' Small triangles of colour crawled slowly across the sea far off to the right.

'And there's Seamus!' Julia pointed over the hedge to the next hay field. Ben had to look very carefully before he could see the black shape weaving its way through the long grass. It was their cast; a tailless Manx, named after Seamus Og, a hero of the Isle of Man. Seamus often followed them when they went for walks.

Ben and Julia stopped when they were out in the middle of the field and approaching the trees. A cuckoo had called from somewhere ahead of them. It called again and the call echoed from the deep recesses of the wood.

'I saw it this morning.'

'Yeh. You said.'

'It came right down to our garden.'

'If it's the same one.'

'Well, I expect it is.'

They climbed the wooden fence and peered into the semi-darkness of the wood. You could hide here and never be found.

The most mysterious feature of this wood was its pool; a very deep pool. About two hundred yards past the first bank of beech trees, on through the oaks and chestnuts, the floor of the wood rose up in a rugged and erratic manner. There was no order or path here. The bare bones of the hill were exposed as extraordinary outcrops of rock. Trees grew at irregular angles. Bracken and fern sprouted from deep clefts between the boulders. An undergrowth of small bushes, stunted trees and brambles made it quite difficult to penetrate this part of the wood. On slightly higher ground, just where you would least expect it, lay the pool, always in semi-shadow, always cold.

'No sign of Mrs B.'s spaceship,' said Ben, leading the way into the woods. Twigs snapped underfoot with little explosions of sound.

From far away the cuckoo called. It had circled around behind them and was now perching in some hedgerow. The woods remained silent. Then a movement caught their attention; a cat appeared momentarily on a rock. It was Seamus. Almost immediately he disappeared again amongst the fronds of bracken.

'Seamus!' Julia called but without really expecting any response.

'Come on, let's see if the orchids are out yet.'

Ben jumped down from the fence into the wood and his sister followed.

'There weren't any last year,' she said.

'That's because we looked for them too late in the summer. I expect they were there.'

Threading their way between the boulders and the tree trunks they tried to remember exactly where the rare Lady's Slipper orchid was to be found. The plant was well established in half a dozen spots in these woods. They liked the limestone in the soil. They were protected by law, but even so, an unscrupulous collector would sometimes dig up a specimen or a vandal would simply pick them as though they were as common as bluebells.

There was no sign of the orchids in any of the places where they searched.

'Perhaps we're too early,' suggested Ben.

'Or maybe someone dug them up.'

'I hope not!' he replied emphatically. 'Come on . . . Let's go on to the pool.'

Disappointed, Ben turned and headed deeper into the wood. For a hundred yards or so there was a discernible path between the trees. It wound up the slope of the hill then petered out and they had to wade through a patch of brittle bracken, last year's growth, brown and scratchy.

They scrambled up a bank over moss-covered rocks, always careful to avoid hidden crevices and old fox holes. Ahead of them a dark crag of rock loomed up amongst the trunks. It was flanked on each side by trees growing at crazy angles out of the bank. More trees grew at the top of the crag.

The pool lay in the shadow of this crag; deep (some would say bottomless), cold and its surface always still.

It was such a dark and overhung place that one would expect the water to be murky, full of leaves and sludge. The mystery about this pool was that it was crystal clear. For as long as anyone in the area could remember, the water was always fresh and ice-cold. Deep down in the hill it was fed by a spring and it was good to drink. Water from the pool cascaded over a flat lip of rock, splashed down a waterfall and ran away through the woods. This small but fast-flowing stream, Filkins Beck, eventually left the woods and rushed down a narrow tree-lined gorge for three miles until it reached the sea. It carried away the leaves which fell into the pool, so that even in autumn it remained as clear as green glass.

Ben got there first. A frown crossed his face. To his left – perhaps twenty feet away – Seamus was sitting on a rock leaning forward with one paw poised to dip. Julia pulled herself up behind him. She gasped and wrinkled up her nose.

The pool was green and entirely full of what looked like pond weed, or some sort of slime. Seamus who had tentatively touched the surface of the pool suddenly pulled back, turned and fled away amongst the trees.

CHAPTER 3

Orchids

'It was disgusting,' said Julia. They had left the ancient trees around the pool behind them and were walking back down through the woods.

'Polluted.'

'Where did all that yucky stuff come from?'

Ben shrugged his shoulders.

'It's never been like that before. Maybe it's some sort of algae, or pond weed.'

'Perhaps there's something blocking the spring deep down. So there's no fresh water getting through?'

'No, look,' Ben pointed. The stream was rushing down through the woods just as fast and full as usual, tumbling and splashing over the rocks from pool to pool. At one spot a small dam had been formed by a tree root and a large slab of rock. Where the water tipped over the lip of the rock there were some long strands of green stuff from the pool. The slime slithered and slipped without hindrance and disappeared down the white splash of the small waterfall.

'Will it all wash away?'

'Hope so,' answered Ben, 'but we don't know what it is or how long it's been there . . . or how fast it grows. But John might know, I'm sure he did some research into algae or slime or something. If it stays we ought to get him to come up and see it.'

They were walking back through the woods by another route following the course of the stream. There were no more large rocks this way and walking was easier. Here was ground elder, wood sorrel and wild garlic. The garlic smelt pungent as they crushed the leaves under foot. As they approached the edge of the wood the dark boles of the trees were silhouetted against the bright landscape beyond – sunlit fields and in the distance the line of the sea. The woodland floor here was rich in leaf mould bedded down deep autumn by autumn. It was springy to walk on.

'Look!' cried Julia. 'A Lady's Slipper orchid.'

'And another.' Ben pointed.

'And another.'

In all they counted five solitary blooms.

'Aren't they beautiful – and sort of proud.' Julia knelt before one of them, tipped its yellow pouch-like petal and looked at it closely. Inside, red spots matched the maroon red of the long sepals and two tiny insects crawled around

29

oblivious of anything beyond their own small semi-enclosed world.

'I'm glad they're still here.' She gazed for some moments at the colourful bloom. It was exotic; it ought to have been in a tropical forest.

Julia stood up. A small bunch of white violets in some undergrowth by the fence caught her eye. She walked over to them and found that there were several clumps.

'Let's pick some for Mum. Remember when we were little she always let us pick a few to make up for not being allowed to pick the orchids?' She gathered ten slender stalks, held them carefully and wrapped them in a twist of moss.

'Come on!' Ben shouted from the fence. 'Let's get back and tell Mrs B. that there aren't any alien spacecraft in Filkins Wood. Think she'll be disappointed?'

They stepped gingerly over some rusty strands of barbed wire, picked their way carefully through a patch of nettles and emerged into the sunlight of the field.

'Race you!' Ben challenged and set off at a fast pace down across the fields. In no time at all they were panting at the back door of the house.

'Beat you!'

'Only just – and anyway I was carrying Mum's white violets.'

'Oh, very heavy!' Ben mocked.

'And Seamus beat you!' she added brightly. The cat was sitting on the kitchen windowsill paws folded as though he hadn't moved all morning.

The back door opened.

'Julia . . .' began her mother, but was interrupted.

'Here, Mum these are for you.' Julia handed her the tiny bunch of flowers in their clump of moss. Her mother took them with a weak smile but seemed distracted.

'Julia,' she began again. 'I'm afraid there's some bad news – it's Blackberry.'

'Blackberry? What's happened?' Julia asked sharply.

'Mrs Lancaster phoned half an hour ago. He's injured one of his legs – staked it, she said.'

Julia remained silent; her face not registering any emotion. Her mother continued:

'She's had the vet to him. But he can't be ridden for at least two months. I am sorry, love.'

She moved to put an arm around her daughter. Julia stared at the ground for a moment and then without a word slipped past her mother into the house. Ben caught his mother's eye and grimaced. He knew how his sister must feel.

'How rotten! Poor Julia,' he muttered and picking up the cat from the windowsill began to stroke it furiously.

Later that afternoon a young man knocked at the back door. Ben recognised him: he was a

31

cub reporter for the local newspaper. He was looking, he said, for Oak Tree Cottage.

'Oh . . . It'll be Mrs Birtwhistle you want,' said Ben. 'Anything to do with the thing she saw last night?'

The man nodded.

'The police always give us a tip-off if there's an interesting story,' he explained.

'I'll show you,' said Ben leading him to the gate. He pointed to where the chimney pots of a cottage could be seen amongst some trees not far down the road.

As the roar of the reporter's noisy exhaust faded Ben turned to go back into the house but then stopped. A different and unusual sound had caught his attention. He had to stand very still cocking his head to one side to catch the distant 'bleep . . . bleep'. It came from the direction of the muddy lane.

Ben jogged up the field to investigate. A police motorbike, all shining chrome and black leather, was parked unattended in the shadows of the overhung lane. The machine, its two-way radio talking to itself and bleeping like an alien, looked stranded and out of place on the rough track. Ben decided to wait and watch. He approached the machine and admired the cluster of dials on its handlebars. He longed for the day when he would be allowed to ride a powerful motorbike.

Ben was bending over the bike when he heard

the sound of heavy feet coming down the lane and he stepped back from the machine just as a very red-faced policeman came round the corner.

'Have you been touching my bike?' he demanded sternly.

'N . . . no. I was just looking.'

Back in his seat the policeman relaxed. In his opinion what Mrs B. had seen was probably no more than someone microlighting by moonlight; and if they were foolish enough to do *that* then they should be left to sort themselves out if they got stuck in a tree. But he had found nothing.

Julia was watching a news programme when Ben walked into the house. He tried to tell her about the bike but she showed not a flicker of interest. He felt sorry for her but slightly irritated, too. Julia was such bad company when she was in a mood.

'Oh, come on,' he said crossly. 'It could be worse.'

'*What* could be worse?' Julia flung back, challenging him.

Ben regretted having spoken. He could see a hefty quarrel brewing and was trying to think of a way to defuse it when a news item on the T.V. caught their attention.

'. . . and somewhere beneath those waves lie the remains of last night's mystery fireball.' The camera, hand-held at the window of a spotter plane, zoomed in on a small marker beacon

33

rising and falling in the Atlantic swell. It had been dropped there in the night by a Nimrod reconnaissance plane scrambled from an air base in Scotland. The pilot had tracked the largest chunk of the fireball, after it had broken up in the stratosphere, on his radar and had marked the spot where it had plunged into the ocean.

The picture on the T.V. changed; a naval recovery vessel filled the screen. It had submarine equipment on board. The fragments of fireball, the commentator explained, had landed on the Continental Shelf where the sea was shallow. There was a very good chance of recovering some of it.

'I had half thought,' said Julia brightening for a moment, 'that perhaps what Mrs B. saw had something to do with the fireball. But I suppose if it crashed into the Atlantic west of Ireland it can't have been.'

Ben shook his head in agreement.

'No, no connection.'

'John is that you? It's Ben. Hi! I was phoning to ask you about your windsurfing board.' Ben was standing on one leg by the dresser in the kitchen. Julia was watching him from the table where she was drinking a cup of hot chocolate before going to bed.

'We've got an extra holiday because the school's closed and Mum says she'll pay for me to have some windsurfing lessons. It'll be much cheaper if I don't have to hire the board too. Is there any chance . . .?' he tailed off and there was a long pause while he listened to the voice at the other end of the line.

'Of course I won't bust it . . . Yeh . . . I promise . . . I'll repaint it for you before you take it away on holiday . . . sure, *great*. Thanks that's fantastic. I'll really look after it I promise . . . yes I know where the sail is.'

'Ask him about the algae stuff,' Julia interrupted.

'Shh! Yes . . . I will . . . sure. Anyway, thanks.' He was nodding hard. 'Hope you can come down at the weekend; we haven't seen you for weeks. Is there any chance? Good . . . good.' He was winding up the conversation when Julia suddenly smacked the table with her hand.

'For heaven's sake, ask him about the slime!' she demanded irritably.

'Oh yes, John, don't hang up. There's something else. Remember the pool in Filkins Wood? It's full of slime or something.' There was a long pause. 'Yes, absolutely full. I chucked a stick in and it landed like it was landing in porridge. It's all green, a bit like a stagnant pond except it isn't stagnant; the stream's still flowing. That's a good idea. See you definitely at the weekend then.' He hung up.

'He says I can borrow his windsurf board.' Ben was looking pleased with himself. 'Tomorrow's going to be great.'

'Its O.K. for you,' muttered Julia.

'Oh yeh, sorry! That's such bad luck about Blackberry. It's really loused things up for you.' Ben tried to sound sympathetic. But Julia was in no mood to receive sympathy. She wasn't ready to talk about her disappointment to anybody.

'Well, what did he have to say about Filkins Pool?' she demanded.

'Oh, he sounded quite interested. He's going to come home at the weekend to have a look.' But then he added darkly, 'I bet he just wants to check on his surfboard.'

'Huh! . . . that's all you care about,' she said crossly and stumped out of the room.

'I'm relying on you, dear.' Julia's mother was standing in the doorway, coat on.

Julia munching her breakfast looked blank. 'What?'

'I'm relying on you,' her mother repeated. 'You know you're the sensible one. There are fish fingers in the deepfreeze and some peas – and there's plenty of bread in the bin. Mrs B. won't be in today. Ben should be back about one. I'll cook us all a proper meal tonight. All right?'

'Come on, Mum!' A shout came from outside. 'I've got my bike in the back of the car and the surfboard's on the roof.'

Dorothy Garstang looked at her daughter for a moment. 'Cheer up I know its hard when plans get spoilt. You could invite Bessy to stay if you like? We could talk about that this evening if you want.'

Julia pulled a face.

'I've gone off Bessy. She's got a boyfriend and she's so boring about it. Honestly it's all she can talk about. Tom this and Tom that.'

'Mum, come on!' Ben shouted again.

'Look dear, I've got to go. We'll think of something for you to do. And darling, *do* give your hair a brush. Bye, love!' Dorothy Garstang threw a kiss to Julia and checking her bag for the car keys left hurriedly.

Julia was despondent; she sat head in hands, elbows on the table. The washing machine churned drearily in the next room. This wasn't the day she had imagined or dreamed about. No horse. No jumping in the field. No riding down the local lanes. No Blackberry to groom or talk to. There's nothing to do, she thought to herself plaintively, and boredom crept up on her like a gloomy friend.

She got up and walked around the room aimlessly; then she stamped her foot crossly and tried to think of something to do.

Filkins Pool! That was it! John was coming home late that night or tomorrow morning. She would collect a sample of the stuff that was polluting the pool to show him as soon as he arrived. The thought of doing something that might please him made her feel better about the day.

What should she collect it in? Jug or bottle? She stood for a moment holding one in each hand, undecided.

Ben returned home a little after one o'clock. He rang his bike bell noisily and lent the bike with a clatter against the wall by the back door.

'What's for lunch?' He burst into the kitchen. 'I'm ravenous – and I only fell into the sea eighty-seven times!'

He was met with silence. He checked the T.V. room and called upstairs: no answer. Perplexed he went to the back door and looked up the garden.

'Julia!'

Still no answer.

Slowly he walked back into the kitchen. He felt a little let down – he wanted to tell somebody about his first morning's windsurfing – and he wanted his lunch; after all, Mum had said that Julia was making it today.

Then he saw the note. It lay on the table half covered by a mug.

Gone to see Bessy in town.
Fish fngers in the deepfreeze.
Something for you in a jug in the fridge.
                                    Julia

She must have passed him in the bus, he thought. But what had she left in a jug? Not some awful soup he hoped. It would be just like her to leave some of his least favourite food for him. He opened the fridge door and his irritation burst into anger.

The jug contained flowers; showy blooms, maroon and yellow. He counted. Five Lady's Slipper orchids.

CHAPTER 4

Slime Moulds

'I've sent her to her room.'

Julia's father sat down heavily in the nearest chair. He had had a tiring day at work and now had returned home to find his family in uproar. Julia apparently had arrived only half an hour before him, by bus; she was in tears. Ben was shouting in that particularly bossy way he had adopted recently, and Dorothy was looking frayed and perplexed. At the eye of this storm, sitting innocently on the table, was a jug of flowers. He recognised them.

'She's so stubborn,' Mr Garstang went on despairingly, 'but I've not known her lie like this before.'

'She always has been stubborn – ever since she could crawl,' agreed his wife. 'But I don't think she tells lies . . . not over anything big. Fibs sometimes, perhaps, but not lies.'

'So why does she go on denying it? It's obvious it must have been *her* who put the orchids in the fridge. She even left a note to tell Ben to look in the jug.' The note still lay on the table. 'But all she says, is that *nothing's* obvious.' He looked at his wife as though expecting some answer. 'So what do we do now?'

'I just don't know – I mean she's been a bit odd all day; I don't think she listened to a word I said to her this morning; she told me she didn't want to see Bessy; but then went into town and spent the afternoon with her; and always she tells one of us if she is going off somewhere. She knows very well it's a family rule; and then she promised to have some lunch ready for Ben when he came back from his first lesson.' She shook her head, 'Perhaps she's more disappointed about Blackberry than I thought. I should have found something else for her to do and not just left her for the day.'

'Suppose she was telling the truth?' suggested Ben. 'She said that she went to collect a sample from the pool to show to John when he comes – and that's what she left in the fridge. But if she *is* telling the truth then how . . .?' He trailed off because at that moment there was a click at the back door and John himself walked in.

'Hi, folks – it's me! I got an earlier train.'

'John, how lovely to see you,' said his mother and gave him a hug.

'Are you all all right? You look a bit gloomy. Have I interrupted something?' He looked at Ben.

41

'It's Julia,' explained his mother, 'she's done something naughty and won't tell us about it.' She pointed at the flowers in the jug and told him all they knew. He took an orchid from the jug and examined it closely. It was perfect in every way. The fleshy tuberous root-system was intact; not a root-fibre missing; not a bruise nor a break. Whoever had dug them up, he observed, had done so immensely carefully and lovingly. There was a good chance that they could be replanted successfully, back in the woods in their native environment. But he was more worried about Julia than he was about the rare orchids.

'It's not like her at all,' he said shaking his head. 'There must be a mistake . . . or maybe there's something wrong. Perhaps she's very upset about something? She might tell me?'

'You can try,' answered his father, 'but you know how she gets if she's in a sulky mood – she goes white in the face and just won't say anything. I can't cope with it; it just makes me angry.'

'We know!' said Ben grimly. 'We heard you!'

'That's enough from you!' replied his father sharply.

'I'll pop up and see her anyway.'

Two minutes later John returned to the kitchen.

'Guess what? She's sound asleep!'

'How's the research?' John's father asked him,

as they sat over a late supper. They had decided to leave Julia sleeping.

'Still deep into fungus?'

'Sort of – I've moved on to slime moulds. They'll be my Ph.D. thesis.'

'Three years studying slime – you can't mean it?' Ben looked incredulous.

'Easily, three years is nothing. There's a whole lifetime's research in slime moulds. They're weird! The ones I'm growing are from caves in the south of France. But you can find them in many cool shady moist places.'

'How about a bag of unwashed games equipment?' asked his mother looking accusingly at Ben.

'Sorry, Mum,' muttered Ben.

'That's not slime mould!' laughed John. 'That's bacteria. Slime moulds are different . . . they are separate living cells rather like tiny amoebas . . . millions of them working together as a team. They're highly organised. They cooperate with each other. When there's plenty of decaying matter about, such as you find in woodland, they all live separately munching away at bacteria . . . like a herd of micro cows. But then, when there's no more bacteria to graze, they swarm together to one spot and form themselves into a single animal, rather like a garden slug. And the slug slithers off to find new pastures!'

'How does each cell know which bit of the slug to become? How does it know if it's at the back end or the front end? Or which way it's going?' quizzed Ben.

'That's one of the mysteries. But there's more. When the team of cells wants to breed, the slug grows a stalk and turns itself into a flower.'

'How charming!' said his mother, passing him the salad bowl.

'Well – it's not all so charming. Even in the microscopic world of slime moulds it's a case of "nature red in tooth and claw", I'm afraid. I'm researching a rare breed which are cannibals. They've evolved a way of surviving by eating other slime moulds.'

'Really charming!' said Ben grinning. 'Then if this stuff in Filkins Pool is one of your slime moulds perhaps it'll turn into giant slugs or something and just slither away?'

'You've been reading too much science fiction! I doubt if it's like anything I'm studying. But we'll see.'

A clean screwtop coffee jar was ideal for collecting a sample of the stuff that was polluting Filkins Pool. Julia watched as John washed it out at the sink. She had fended off conversation and stayed in her shell all through breakfast. With her thick hair well forward across her face she managed to shut out the rest of the world. They didn't believe her and so they had no right to talk to her. She still felt resentful and angry.

The jug of orchids was still at the centre of the

table. Julia kept eyeing them. She could still feel the shock of being accused of doing something she would *never* do – and of nobody believing her when she denied it. *Somebody*, she thought, must have come into the kitchen after she had left and before Ben got back. But who and why?

When it looked as though John and Ben were about to leave, Julia stood up, lifted the jug of blooms from the table and, without speaking, walked out of the back door. She had listened to them talking about replanting the orchids in the woods. No one was going to deprive her of the chance to show that *she* cared about them too, whatever they thought she had done.

Still not talking, Julia walked ahead of her brothers and didn't stop until she had crossed the field and entered the muddy lane. John caught up with her first.

'Help!' she suddenly whispered.

John looked at her questioningly.

'Look, it's Mr Jackson and his wife.' The retired primary school headmaster and Mrs Jackson were walking down the lane towards them. The white haired Mr Jackson with his limp and a stick was well known in the district as a keen environmentalist. To be caught by him with rare wild orchids would be unimaginably dreadful.

Julia felt a rush of gratitude as her brother quickly took the jug from her, grabbed the pullover which Ben was wearing draped across his shoulders and wrapped it carefully over the orchids and the jug. With that he led on at a fast pace up the lane. The three of them greeted the Jacksons effusively but without stopping.

Julia grinned. The silence between them was broken.

When they reached Filkins Wood, they skirted the woods following the fence round to the right.

'Somewhere about here I guess,' said Ben stepping over some collapsed fencing.

He was right. After taking only a few steps into the wood they came to the exact spot where they had seen the orchids. Much to Julia's delight, the five plants were still there, just as they had left them.

'Anyone remember a trowel?' asked John, and laughed as their faces fell. He then produced one with a flourish from his jacket pocket.

'Now where?' He looked around for a suitable place and started digging. First he had to scrape away layers of dead leaves to uncover the rich loamy soil.

'This should do,' he said, and cleared four more spots chosen at random.

'Got to be careful not to make them look like a park flower bed.'

Julia handed him the orchids one by one from the jug. Each one was carefully positioned and then gently bedded in. The soil smelt of mushrooms. Julia's hands had been tainted with the same smell after collecting the sample from

Filkins Pool the day before. It was subtle and easily overpowered by the more familiar smells of the earth.

'There!' John stood up. 'They look as though they've always been here.' And it was true.

Ben set off deeper into the woods. 'Come on!' he called back.

Minutes later he was pulling his way between and up and over the last of the rocks. They saw him steady himself against a crooked oak tree.

'Julia!' he called without turning.

She reached him puffing; stopped and said nothing. The pool was quite devoid of slime; the water clear as crystal.

CHAPTER 5

Silver Fish and White Violets

The three of them stood silent and John looked at Julia and Ben in turn. 'Is this by any chance a late April fool? Mysterious orchids in the fridge and non-existent slime – what's going on?'

Julia stepped forward to peer into the deep pool. 'It was clogged two days ago – absolutely clogged. It was like thick soup. And some of it was all over those rocks.' She pointed across the pool. 'And this was where I knelt down to fill the bottle.' She indicated a part of the bank between two rocks. 'I was frightened of falling in and wanted something to hold on to – there aren't any trees easy enough to grab, they are either too big or too far . . .' She trailed off as she noticed to her surprise that John was leaning against a tree that would have been ideal to hang on to. Why hadn't she noticed it before? It was a straight, ten foot, silver birch tree, growing from the very edge of the pool. All the other trees around the pool were bent and crooked;

ancient oaks and rowan and a giant ash growing from the top of the rock face opposite.

'A bottle?' John was asking her. 'I thought you said you put the stuff in that jug?'

'Oh no – I got it in a wine bottle and then poured it into the jug to put it in the fridge. The bottle was too big unless I put it on its side and I couldn't find a cork.'

Julia's face suddenly lit up.

'There was some left!' she exclaimed excitedly. 'The slime wouldn't all go into the jug – there must have been at least a quarter of a bottle left over.'

'So?'

'I didn't know what to do with it so I put the bottle outside the back door behind the hydrangea bush. It'll still be there!'

'But what happened to all this lot?' John asked waving at the pool. 'If it's vanished here maybe it's vanished from your bottle too.'

'Perhaps that rain storm washed it away in the night – it rained very heavily,' suggested Ben. 'But it can't all have reached the sea. We could walk downstream to see if any of it has got caught up on the way.'

He gave a start and leaned over to stare down into the pool. He thought he had seen a movement. 'There's something? . . . Hey look! There's something down there.' He pointed. For a moment their vision was obscured. A gust of wind blowing down through the trees stirred the surface of the pool; a gauze of ripples spread from one side to the other turning the water temporarily to frosted glass.

John, holding to the slender trunk of the silver birch tree, leant out over the pool; Julia and Ben knelt on the bank and peered down waiting for the surface of the water to settle. It quickly returned to its usual smooth glass-like state.

Reflections of the trees surrounding the pool and the small irregular patches of sky between the branches made it hard to see into the water. Julia shaded her eyes, trying to penetrate beyond the reflections. She could just make out the shapes of rocks at least twenty feet down; bottle brown shadows. She swept her eye out into the darker, deeper, parts of the pool.

'There!' Ben jabbed his finger downwards.

'Yes! . . . I saw it!' exclaimed John.

The water in the pool seemed to heave slightly, to swell, lapping and splashing at the rocks around the edge. Then it settled again, steady, unruffled.

'But what?' Julia leant further forward.

'It can't be . . .' began Ben, but trailed off.

A huge dark shadow had moved in the depths. They had all seen it.

'If it's a fish it's *enormous* . . . must be well over ten feet long,' whispered John.

They remained motionless, their hearts pounding.

Whatever it was did not move again. But

over to the left, where the roots of an oak tree could clearly be seen gripping the rocks not many feet beneath the surface, a small fish had appeared. It was the size of a two-pound trout.

'Now that *is* a fish,' said Ben pointing.

The fish was silver and very sleek. It turned and darted across the pool revealing rainbow colours on its underside. It turned again and swam back in a more leisurely manner.

'What sort is it?' queried John. 'You're the fisherman in the family.'

'I've never seen one like it before,' Ben replied.

The fish headed slowly out to the centre of the pool and then with a flurry and a flick it shot towards the surface like a torpedo. With water slipping from its tail it leapt six feet into the air somersaulting twice and was caught for a fraction of a second in a dapple of sunlight. It landed back in the pool with a clean 'plop'. A flick of the tail sent it gliding across towards the underwater roots of the oak tree.

'I'm sure it's not an English fish. Someone must have released it from an aquarium.'

The fish, meanwhile, had turned and was returning in their direction.

'Is it looking at you?' whispered Julia.

Ben and the fish eyed each other for some moments.

'Have a go at tickling it,' suggested John.

Quickly Ben made a grab and raised the fish before the astonished eyes of John and Julia. It could easily have leapt back into the water if it had wanted to.

'Just look at those markings!' whispered John, who had crouched down beside Ben. A line of black marks ran down its silvery side from its gills to its tail; they looked as though they had been drawn with a fine brush by a Chinese artist.

'They look like Chinese writing! This is the weirdest fish I have ever seen.'

The fish seemed to suffer no distress from being out of the water. It lay still and heavy in Ben's two hands, like a friendly pet, dripping into the pool.

'What shall I do with it?' asked Ben bewildered. His question was soon answered and he let out a shout of pain.

'Ow!'

He stood up sharply, clutching his hands together. With a flip the fish had leapt from his grasp and was gone. Ben shook his right hand and grimaced in anguish. Two drops of blood had appeared.

'It had sharp fins like a stickleback on its belly – it suddenly opened them.' He licked the ball of his thumb which was bleeding quite badly and peered into the pool. 'Monster!' he shouted. The fish was diving deeper with apparent purpose. They watched as it disappeared into the darkness of the depths.

'Let's see,' said Julia examining Ben's hand.

There were two wounds. 'They look nasty . . . you better put a plaster on when we get back.'

'I've been thinking,' said John slowly. 'I reckon that the slime you saw and the fish are connected. Whoever released the fish into the pool *also* put some sort of pond weed in with it . . . maybe something it eats. Whatever it was spread fast – perhaps the minerals in Filkins water were ideal for it. But then it grew too well, clogged the whole pool, and died. Then it sank. A great mass of waterlogged vegetation. And that's what we saw moving down there. I expect the spring keeps disturbing it so that it moves about like a sort of submarine raft.'

Filkins Wood was full of surprises that day. They followed the stream down through the woods for about half a mile and made another strange discovery. Ahead of them they saw what looked at first like snow or a heavy coating of hoar frost between the trees. They walked closer and then all they could do was stand and stare. White violets: millions of them carpeted the woodland floor. Normally white violets were quite difficult to find growing in small bunches. Swathes of them spread between the trees.

On their way home something happened which Julia was to recall at a much later date and in much stranger circumstances. They had decided not to follow the road back past Mrs B.'s cottage but to cut back up across the fields.

As they were walking along the lower side of a field of hay, a cuckoo suddenly broke cover from the hedgerow and flew low over their heads. It brushed so close they could hear the wind in its feathers. Ben fixed his eye on the spot in the hedge where the bird had emerged; a hawthorn bush. When he investigated, he found a nest: a neat bundle of twigs and grass knitted into a forking branch of the hawthorn. Fresh green moss and downy feathers indicated that the nest was new. Holding back the sharp twigs and brambles from his face he peered inside; five tiny eggs nestled in the soft down. Four were pale blue and each no larger than a fingernail; the fifth was a little bigger and mottled green-grey; a cuckoo's egg.

Ben kept his hands well away from the nest so as to leave no smell; the scent of a human hand could make a bird desert. John and Julia peered in turn at the delicate clutch of eggs; so fine, so fragile. A hedgesparrow, known locally as a dunnock, rasped its alarm call and fluttered in agitation in the next bush.

Julia was troubled by the cuckoo's egg. The other four chicks would be cruelly kicked out of the nest, by the interloper, to die in the ditch. It was four to one – even before considering the parents and their feelings. It was obvious to Julia that they should not leave the cuckoo's egg where it was.

John shook his head decisively. It would be

quite improper to interfere with the course of nature.

Julia remained silent. Surely, people had a duty to prevent suffering. They always stopped Seamus from playing with a mouse if he caught one – and that was supposed to be natural; part of a cat's nature. Suddenly it was all too much for her and she burst into tears. Ben looked at her in astonishment. She always hated it when he stared at her like that and she swung her hair so that it curtained her face.

It was a release and a relief to cry. Everything had been bottled up for so long. First the disappointment about Blackberry and then the terrible misunderstanding about the orchids; she still didn't understand what had happened, but at least Ben knew now that they were not the same blooms as the ones they had first seen together. Now, on top of it all, the thought of the hedgesparrow losing its babies was more than she could bear.

Ben would never understand, she thought, how nice it could be to cry. Turning away from her brothers she set off down the hedgerow and arrived home before them.

The large Bollinger wine bottle was just where Julia had said she had left it; propped against the drain pipe behind the hydrangea bush by the back door. With relief and fascination John found that there was more than enough slime for a sample. The stuff had bred and spread. The drain was covered in a rich green layer; the wall of the house up to half a metre was festooned in strands; the ground around the hydrangea was smothered. The bottle itself had disappeared beneath a glistening glutinous eruption, which had spewed from its neck like lava from a volcano.

John took samples in three separate jars, just to be sure. He examined the slime closely: it was completely new to him. Unfortunately the man at the university, who ought to be able to identify the slime, was abroad and wouldn't be back for a fortnight. But John promised to phone as soon as he had some news.

Mr Garstang fixed a hosepipe to the kitchen tap and washed the remaining slime down the drain. A generous dose of bleach followed. He wanted no wet rot, dry rot, fungus rot or any other rot getting into the house.

Whatever the slime was had an incredible life force. It led John to wonder again about what had happened to all the stuff in Filkins Pool. If a small quantity left in a bottle could grow into all this in such a short time, then what would happen if any of it got into the sea?

CHAPTER 6

Hallelujah

Ben stood on the shingle and looked up at the clouds. There was a light breeze; it was a good day for windsurfing. He looked down at the sea and remembered the last thing John had said before leaving. 'Let's hope none of the slime gets into the sea. It might like salt water!' He tried to imagine the sea clogged up like Filkins Pool and shivered.

It was a fortnight now since John had gone back to his university. It was time they heard from him, Ben thought, as he made his way down the beach between the picnickers. A salvation band were playing loudly to a group of children, strumming guitars, shaking tambourines and shouting 'Hallelujah'.

He walked on to the sand and along the beach towards the huts where the windsurf boards were kept. They lay chained together for security. Some of the boards had been untied and one was being carried down to the water's edge. He checked that he had the key to his padlock in the pocket of his jeans.

It was Saturday afternoon and he had already been windsurfing once that day. It had become an obsession. He was either skimming across the sea or talking about doing it or else dreaming of it.

As he walked back up across the shingle to the top of the beach he noticed a boy sitting crosslegged staring out to sea. Something about him was extraordinarily familiar. Ben guessed he was a couple of years older than himself. He had wild blond hair, quite long, untamed: it kept blowing across in front of his eyes. His face wore a serious preoccupied expression. He wore an old pair of shorts and an oil-stained tee-shirt which looked as though they might have been found when beachcombing. He had no shoes.

'Hi!' Ben called as he walked up across the beach in front of him.

The boy raised a hand and gave a hesitant smile. Ben paused and then turned towards him. 'Can you windsurf?'

'No – but I can swim.' He spoke slowly like someone trying out new words for the first time. 'And I expect I could windsurf too if I tried . . . but I don't have a . . . a . . . surfboard.'

'It takes a bit of learning,' said Ben. 'I fell in an awful lot before I got it right!'

'I know!' the boy laughed. 'I saw you!'

Not wanting to be caught looking put out by this remark, Ben picked up a pebble and with a swing hurled it towards the sea. It landed on the wet sand as a wave receded.

'What's your name?' he asked. But the boy had jumped to his feet, picked up another pebble and with an effortless flick had launched it on a curving path up into the sky. Ben watched it make a neat small splash well out beyond the forth line of waves.

'Wow!' Ben said in admiration and then repeated his question.

There was a long pause as the boy looked straight at him without answering. Ben tried once more. He was beginning to feel rather awkward. Perhaps the boy really only understood a little English after all. 'Have you *got* a name?' he tried joking.

'Oh . . . Yes . . . but no one has asked me before.' There was another long pause, as though he were trying to make up his mind on something. 'It's Hallelujah,' he said cautiously.

'Hallelujah?'

'Yes . . . Hallelujah!' He spoke now with conviction.

'Are you one of that lot?' Ben nodded in the direction of the hymn-singing salvation band who were handing out small white pamphlets to the sunbathers.

'No . . . but that's my name.' His smile was broad and confident now; and very engaging.

A funny name thought Ben. But he didn't say so. 'Well I don't fall in much now,' he said. 'In fact you could say I've been making great strides on the sea!' It was a joke he'd repeated too often at home. Hallelujah just looked perplexed.

'You walk on the sea, too?'

'Oh never mind.' Ben turned away. 'I'm going to see what the wind's like out there today. Cheerio!' and then he added. 'Nice to talk to you . . . See you again some time.'

'Yes, I hope so,' Hallelujah replied with his friendly smile. He sat down again on the shingle. Then he called, 'I'll watch to see if you fall in! Bet you do!' he taunted.

Ben was wearing his swimming trunks under his jeans. He quickly stripped, folded his clothes and put them beneath a large stone. He rather liked the boy. But there was something about him, something uncannily familiar; it had been rather like meeting an older version of himself. He had the strange feeling that he knew him and yet he didn't know him at all. It left him curious but slightly uneasy.

Ben pushed the board out into the water. The sea was relatively calm. Regular waves were creaming up over the sand, pulling at pebbles as they ran back again. He waded out deeper, lay on the board and paddled it away from the beach, its sail floating alongside. How nice it would be, he thought, just to lie here in the warm sun. Then he remembered the challenge from the boy on the beach. For some reason he valued the boy's opinion. Bracing himself for action, he pushed himself up from the horizontal, took hold of the rope and, tugging at it, attempted to pull the sail out of the water and into a vertical position. By this time he had drifted back to the shore and was facing the wrong way. Very carefully and deliberately, so as not to give the impression of falling in, he climbed down and pushed himself once more out into the waves. This time he stood up quickly, pulled up the sail and caught the breeze. In a moment he was gliding away from the beach. He turned his head feeling well in control and waved back at the shore. Hallelujah, still sitting cross-legged, waved back.

A power boat sped past with a water skier in tow. Ben gripped his sail bar tight and waited for the impact of the waves in the wake of the speeding craft. He felt exhilarated as he rode them without mishap. Absorbed now, he forgot how tired he had been. The wind rose slightly and he began to skim across the sea with ease. Two other windsurfers slid past him making their way back to the shore. One was a girl. She called across to him and he nodded back with a broad grin when he recognised her. It was Helen from his form at school.

Very soon there was nothing between Ben and the flat horizon, apart that is from a smudge of smoke from a tanker far out to sea. Looking in that direction he could imagine himself totally alone in the middle of the ocean. It felt grand to be riding the sea so successfully and a thrill of achievement ran through him. He, the board and the pulling sail were all one, working together in harmony. The beach had shrunk to a narrow line in the distance; sunbathers appeared the size of ants. The town seemed a toy town; rising curves of fields and woods spread out behind the town to the line of moors on the horizon. There was no sign of Helen and her friend or any other windsurfers for that matter.

The breeze kept his skin dry and the sun was warm on his shoulders. He let the board slide on straight across the sea. He scanned the horizon inland. Looking further down the coast he could make out the fields that lay beyond his house; the house itself was hidden in a slight hollow behind a low shoulder of land. Further inland he could see a dark line of trees which he judged to be Filkins Wood. His thoughts went to Filkins Pool. That fish was a real mystery. There was nothing like in his *Guide to European Freshwater Fish*. His hand still hurt slightly where the fish had wounded him in the muscle of his thumb. Holding the sail bar with his left hand for a moment he examined his other hand: he could still see the mark where the fish had pierced him with its spiked fin.

High up over the moors beyond Filkins Wood a large cumulo-nimbus cloud was boiling up into the sky like a giant white cauliflower: the sort of cloud that brings thunderstorms in summer.

It was already reaching up towards the stratosphere, brilliant white in the afternoon sun, its edges clear cut against the deep blue sky. At its top, the cloud was spreading out like a giant's anvil. It was beautiful.

Ben studied the cloud for a while: the sky beneath it was turning black. Mare's tails, wisps of high cirrus, lay innocently across the horizon to the south and south west. The wind changed direction though Ben did not notice it at first. A squall of wind swept across the waves. It caught his sail just as he was trying to change direction to head back for the shore. For a moment he struggled holding himself upright. But, just as the squall passed by, he found himself falling backwards and pulling the sail over on top of himself.

'Damn!' he spluttered as he came to the surface. He was too far from shore, he hoped, for Hallelujah to have seen the mishap. He hung on to the surfboard for a few moments and then heaved himself up on to it. His intention to stand up immediately and pull the sail out of the water was frustrated by another squall of wind, which whipped spray off a passing wave and drenched his face once more. The wave rolled on. As he sunk into the trough between that wave and the next one Ben realized that he could see nothing of the land at all.

Ben clung to his board and waited for the next wave to carry him up again. Desperately he tried to get his bearings; land he guessed must be where the horizon was darkest. But not even a pencil line gave any hint of its presence or direction. The horizon had closed in and become blurred as sheets of rain draped themselves across the seascape.

Squalls of wind came irregularly but often. The air was filled with salty spray. Then it began to rain and the rain flattened the crests of the great waves as they rolled past him. It stung his hands and face terribly; and then he understood why – little tiny pellets of ice were bouncing off his surfboard. The rain was partly hail.

Everything was grey now; the sea, the sky, the rain.

A flash of lightning and a clap of thunder brought him quickly to a crouching position. With blue hands he heaved the sail free of the water. But almost immediately another squall of wind smacked him down again. Ben dragged himself out once more and clutching the board realized how exhausted he felt. He was no longer in control and suddenly he felt very frightened. The sea had become an enemy: he might have been a bit of discarded driftwood for all it cared.

A wave washed over the board, as he clung to it, leaving strings of seaweed. Mixed with the seaweed were strands of green slime.

'Bother Ben!' Julia thought to herself.

She had waited in the rain at the bus stop, but he had not turned up at the agreed time. The bus had come and gone.

Julia had spent most of the afternoon with Betty and a few friends. They had taken shelter in a café during the worst of the storm, making a few cups of coffee last a long time. Now the thunder had moved out to sea but it was still raining and she was soaked. The sea was dark and very rough. Heavy waves pounded the shingle dragging it down with a roar and then flinging it back again. The horizon was still smudged with rain, but there were no boats visible in any direction. The crests of the waves were white with foam. She pitied anyone out in a boat in a sea like this . . .

Three people were standing at the top of the beach throwing stones out into the surf: two boys and a girl. She walked towards them and recognised the girl. It was Helen from Ben's class. The boys were local but Julia didn't know their names.

'Hi, Helen!' she called. 'Have you seen Ben?'

'No . . . well, not since earlier this afternoon. He was windsurfing when we came in. But he'd have seen the storm coming and given up long ago. He might be sheltering in the hut along the beach,' she pointed to the huts several hundred yards away.

'That's what I thought,' replied Julia.

The hut looked far from hopeful. It was locked

as she had feared; and there was no sign of Ben anywhere. Fed up and feeling just a little bit desperate she scanned the sea but could see nothing but the wild waves; she gazed intently along the beach in both directions but could see nobody; even Helen and her friends had disappeared.

Julia went over to see if she could recognise Ben's surfboard from amongst the rest but they all looked the same to her. She was turning away to leave when suddenly she froze: there in front of her on the beach were Ben's shoes; beneath a rock beside them his jeans and shirt — folded. She looked at the sea. It was terrible and empty.

The shifting shingle dragged heavily at Julia's feet as she tried to sprint back along the beach. The loose sand was no better.

She comforted herself with the thought that Ben was a strong swimmer. He must be all right. He *must* be.

Breathless, she ran up off the beach through the car park and headed straight for the café. Helen and her two friends were just leaving as she arrived.

'Ben's not back,' she gasped, 'his shoes are on the beach . . . and his jeans . . . I think he must be . . .'

Helen's reaction was immediate.

'Quick – the lifeguards.' She dashed across the road to the public phone box.

'But we've got no change left,' one of her friends called after her, as they followed.

'No need – it's an emergency call,' she shouted back over her shoulder. Then she added, 'Oh damn!'

A large middle-aged lady was chatting on the phone. 'Please – this is a real emergency . . . may we use the phone?'

The lady turned to her sharply. 'There's another phone in Lowther Street . . . You've got young legs,' she said crossly; and, shifting her weight, swung even more of her back towards Helen.

'The café – they've got a phone,' suggested one of Helen's friends.

The manager of the café allowed them all to cram into his office. Helen gave all the details.

Within a few minutes they heard the sound of a helicopter in the distance; it flew low over the town with a heavy wuthering roar and on out to sea. Julia, much against her will, began to tremble and shake. Helen put an arm round her.

'Hey! . . . Don't worry! . . . You're cold, you're wet, you've had a shock, you've been running. It's not surprising you're shivering! Ben's a strong swimmer remember – he'll be all right.'

'I know,' sniffed Julia, 'but they said that man who drowned last week was a strong swimmer, too.'

'Yes, but he'd been drinking . . . silly fool. Come on, let's phone your mum.'

'I'll do it,' Julia insisted firmly. She dialled and waited but the number was engaged. She dialled again. Her mother answered and Julia tried not to sound upset. The big difficulty was knowing what to say first. She wanted to avoid causing alarm – and anyway she thought, clinging to a last desperate hope, perhaps Ben was at home after all.

'Mum – I'm at the café . . . We can't find Ben,' she paused waiting for some prompting to tell her what to say next, but then she stumbled on, 'they've sent a helicopter out to look for him . . . we don't know if he came in from windsurfing or not. He was out there before the storm . . . Helen saw him . . . but we haven't seen him since . . . all right I'll stay here until you come,' then she quickly corrected herself. 'No I won't . . . I'll be down on the beach with the others . . . O.K. see you then.'

The manager of the café had put four cups of coffee for them on his desk. He waved away Helen's offer to pay for them next time they came in. After gulping the coffee they quickly left.

It was a shock for Ben to see a face staring at him from inside a curling wave. As the wave rolled past the face broke surface and a swimmer swam towards him with powerful strokes. Taking hold of the windsurf board with one hand, the swimmer wiped the sea water from his face

68

with the other and ran his fingers back through his soaking hair.

Ben recognised him with astonishment.

'Hi!' said the swimmer with a grin. 'So! . . . you fall in!'

Ben nodded with a wry and tired smile. 'Yeh . . . you win . . . But you *swam* out in this storm?'

'I swim . . . I not walk on waves!'

'I'm glad to see you.' It was an understatement.

Some rain was still falling, but the sky was not as dark as it had been. Apart from one distant rumble, there had been no thunder for at least a quarter of an hour. The centre of the storm had moved away out to sea. But the waves were still menacing, breaking into foam at their tops, drenching Ben again and again as he lay on the board, unnerved and fearing to make any more attempts to raise the sail.

'How did you find me?'

'Not difficult. Come on, you're cold. You must get your body working again. Can you swim now? If I help you? It's warmer in the water.'

Ben gave a slight nod. 'I think so.' He eased himself off the board and into the water and clutching on it as though it were a large float began to kick his legs.

'I'll be all right. I'm O.K.'

'We must get rid of the sail,' said Hallelujah.

'It's no good trying to use it in such rough sea. Like this, it's just a drag.'

'Hope John won't mind too much,' Ben said, as they unhooked the sail, 'I'll have to buy him a new one.'

'John? Who is John?'

'My brother. This is his board.'

'Well, I expect he'd rather have a brother than a sail. We have long way to go and you very tired.'

The yellow and white sheet of plastic, with its mast and steering bar, floated free. It rose and fell beside them as waves ran beneath it. Now they could make better progress against the sea.

Hallelujah pushed the front of the board round through more than 90 degrees. 'This way,' he said simply, and began to pull the board along beside him as he swam. Ben was perplexed; he was sure that they must now be heading out to sea.

'Land's *that* way?' He waved back to his left.

Hallelujah shook his head and laughed.

'If we go *that* way, we'll be swimming all night and all tomorrow. Come on! Swim hard! Get your blood moving again. If you get too tired, tell me and I'll push while you float on the board.'

There was nothing Ben could do but trust this extraordinary boy.

A few minutes later Ben had to struggle up on to the board with agonising cramp in his right leg. He gritted his teeth and growled in his throat against the pain. They massaged his calf vigorously and he flexed the leg as much as he could until the tight knot of muscle relaxed. With relief he felt the pain ease.

'Come on!' commanded Hallelujah.

Ben slipped back into the sea. He felt disorientated and still had the worrying feeling that they were heading in the wrong direction.

A patch of seaweed got caught up on the front of the windsurfboard: long brown slippery thongs, with the sort of pods you could pop. Ben swam forward and pulled it free. He noticed that entwined with the seaweed there were some more green strands of slime: stuff that he had seen before. Was it the same as he had seen in Filkins Pool?

CHAPTER 7

Look-alikes

The helicopter was circling far out to sea. The afternoon was lighter; the clouds were lifting and the rain had stopped completely. The sea was still rough: white crests capped the waves.

Julia stopped jogging, to have a breather, and pointed to the horizon. The helicopter was hovering very low and close to the waves.

'They've found something,' she exclaimed.

'Let's hope it's Ben,' answered Helen, who was standing beside her. The four of them, after running down to the beach from the café, had found it impossible just to stand around staring out at the empty sea. So they had set off at a fast jog along the top of the beach above the line of sloping shingle. The tide was high. The town was now a couple of miles behind them.

'Ben's yellow and white sail is very bright . . . I expect they've found him,' said Helen.

The helicopter had been hovering in the same position for some minutes. But then very slowly it began to circle the spot flying low, just clear of the waves.

'I wish we could see!' Julia muttered in exasperation. The coast was very low here: she wished there was a tree or a cliff they could climb to get a better view. The helicopter was circling wider and wider, but still very slowly and methodically. Obviously the pilot had discovered something. If it was Ben's bright sail then why was he still searching the area?

All they could do was go on running until they came to some low cliffs. The beach was covered with large boulders where the cliffs had collapsed. It was just beyond here that Filkins Beck finally poured down a narrow ravine and into the sea. At high tide it was a difficult and dangerous scramble to get anywhere along the shore by the cliffs.

Julia was worrying about her mother: she had promised to wait for her down on the beach but they were now well out of sight of the town. The search for Ben felt hopeless. The coast appeared completely deserted. They were debating whether or not to turn back, when one of Helen's friends pointed to the rocks ahead of them where Filkins Beck ran into the sea.

'Look!'

A figure in shorts was stooping between two large boulders.

'Let's ask if he's seen Ben.'

They made their way carefully over the slippery rocks until close enough to shout above the noise of the sea. The roar of the waves made it hard to hear anything else.

'Hallo-o! Hallooo-o!' called Helen.

Eventually the person heard and looked up.

'Have you seen . . .' began Helen and then, her face lighting up, said 'It's Ben!' She hesitated suddenly uncertain. At that moment a second figure staggered to his feet and leant against the rock.

'It's Ben!' shrieked Julia.

'Are you all right?' she called as she scrambled over another barnacle encrusted boulder.

Ben waved.

He sat down again on his surf board and was looking exhausted and blue with cold when she reached him. She gave him a hug and felt both angry and relieved at the same time.

'We thought you'd drowned . . . why didn't you come inshore when the storm started? They're looking for you out there now.' She pointed to the horizon where the helicopter was still circling.

'I'm OK,' he answered weakly trying to smile. 'If Hallelujah hadn't turned up I *might* have drowned.' He introduced the person beside him.

'Hallellujah . . . my sister Julia . . . Julia this is Hallellujah.'

Julia's mouth fell open rather rudely. Hallellujah looked just like her brother! Helen, who had just

74

joined her, was still staring at him in surprise. She had thought that he *was* Ben at first.

Julia quickly shut her mouth and reached out to shake hands with the stranger. He didn't seem to know what to do at first but then, realising, took her hand awkwardly. Julia was lost for words and could only mumble 'Hallo!' and 'Thanks!'

Hallellujah was older and slightly taller than her brother, she decided – like Ben might be in a couple of years' time. He had the same broad cheekbones and wide mouth; the same coloured hair, blond. It was uncanny. Hallellujah's eyes mirrored Ben's exactly – the same grey-green and the same shape. Apart from a faint unshaven shadow about his jaw, his skin was remarkably pale and fresh-looking and quite unblemished: not a spot anywhere, unlike Ben who usually had two or three on his chin.

'How do you feel?' one of the boys was asking Ben. 'Can you walk . . . or shall we carry you back to town on the surf board?' He removed his jumper and made Ben put it on.

'Hi! . . . I'm Helen. You're a hero! Are you a relative? You look just like Ben,' she said, stating the obvious. 'Were you swimming in that storm? Or did you have a windsurf board too?'

Hallellujah shook his head, then nodded, then hesitated, then laughed.

'No . . . not relative. Yes, I was swimming. I saw Ben needed help so I swam.' He spoke slowly testing each word cautiously. He sounded very matter-of-fact.

'Well, you deserve a medal,' said Helen.

'A medal?' he queried.

Ben refused to be treated as a stretcher case, though he did accept help over the slippery rocks. They took turns in carrying his surf board; except for one of the boys who ran on ahead to call off the search. The helicopter was still busily flying round and round, away out to sea near the horizon, like a dragonfly skimming a pond.

The unexpected arrival of Hallellujah in their family life changed everything for Julia. Her parents were so grateful to him for saving Ben's life that they took to him immediately; and he looked so like their son that he seemed part of the family as soon as he stepped over the threshold. They assumed, from the hesitant way he used words, that he was a young foreign student and since he seemed to have nowhere in particular to stay they were more than happy to offer him John's room and he readily accepted. In their flush of gratitude they gave no thought to how long he might want to stay.

Julia had taken to calling him Hal. 'We can't go on calling you Hallellujah,' she had said within an hour of meeting him and he had happily agreed with a grin.

Hal had great charm and an air of mystery.

76

His rather strange slow English dried up almost completely when asked questions about himself. Yes, he had come a long way; and it was a long story which he would tell them one day was all he would say. The Garstangs probed no further; he inspired in them a great respect for his privacy. Only Julia's father felt a twinge of uneasiness. A young foreign student, travelling without money and apparently no possessions or passport, was a bit suspicious, he thought. But then it seemed ungracious to think it and deep down he shared his family's instinctive feeling that Hal could be trusted. He, like the others, was riveted by Hal's appearance: if he had been two or three years younger he could have been his son's identical twin.

Ben had been more exhausted than he liked to admit when they got him home; but he revived over supper and became very talkative. He made it sound as though he had been shipwrecked in mid Atlantic. Julia did at one point remind him quietly, however, that Hal had swum through the same heavy sea.

Before supper was over, Ben slowly flopped asleep over his plate. No sooner had Ben gone to bed than the phone rang. It was John. Dorothy Garstang had answered it and she launched into a long account of Ben's drama in the storm. With a sidelong glance at Hal she explained how he had been saved by a remarkable boy who looked just like him. When she started talking about the surf board Julia interrupted her with a loud whisper.

'Don't tell him about the sail, Mum . . . I'm sure Ben wants to tell him himself.' She knew Ben would hate John to know. Her mother ignored her and continued with all the details.

'Julia,' she said finally, holding out the phone to her. 'He wants to speak to you . . . something about the slime being very exciting.'

Julia took the phone from her eagerly. 'Hi! . . . How are you? . . . I've tried phoning lots of times but you're never in . . . so what's this about the slime? I thought perhaps you'd forgotten all about it.'

The slime, John said, was the most remarkable organism that they had ever had in the laboratory. Its extraordinary nature had remained hidden at first; in a test tube it neither developed nor withered. In two weeks of close observation it showed no signs of growth or decay; it was healthy and living but totally inert despite their attempts to make it react and do something. They had heated it slowly to over 100 degrees centigrade and then frozen it to minus 50 degrees. It had remained unaffected by these extreme conditions.

Under the microscope the slime appeared to have a uniquely complex structure having, amongst other surprises, a triple nucleus to each miniscule cell. Nothing on earth had ever been seen like it before.

The slime had only begun to reveal its true potential, however, when a small sample was set aside in a separate test tube of water and fed with a powerful weedkiller to investigate how quickly it would take up the poison and in what manner it would decay. The slime consumed the toxin and flourished! Further experiments all revealed the same amazing ability. Any pollutants suspended in water, however poisonous, were attacked destroyed and consumed by the slime.

'Is it dangerous?' asked Julia.

John assured her that as far as they could tell it posed no threat to people (they had all been handling it in the lab) or to any other living thing.

Professor Duckworth, John's boss, was so excited by their discoveries he had dropped all other research in the labs – even some sponsored by the government. All their experiments confirmed the almost unbelievable conclusion that the slime could consume, in a matter of hours, concentrated solutions of the most toxic wastes produced by any factory in Europe. Properly developed the slime could be the answer to the world's pollution problems. It was a biological miracle.

But the strangest part of the story to Julia's mind was that overnight the slime had changed its form dramatically. A sample had been placed in a test tube with a particularly nasty form of industrial waste, which contained a high proportion of deadly mercury. It had been left for twelve hours. The following morning the test tube was found to contain nothing but a small amount of pure water, as pure as anything you could buy in a bottle. A tell-tale track had been found leading away from the test-tube rack, as though left by something like a large slug or snail. The trail crossed the top of the lab bench, descended a leg to the floor, made its way straight over the floor towards another bench where it climbed again and came to an end at a dish which contained a sample of mud taken from a village pond. The mud in the dish had completely vanished and in its place was a beautiful miniature garden of waxy green leaves and tiny star-like yellow flowers. Nobody could identify them. The microscope revealed that they were made of the same cells as the slime. Julia was reminded of her orchids.

'John doesn't know what it is . . . but he says it's a mutation. It eats anything and can turn itself into flowers!' she told her family. 'John is going to come down in a couple of days with two of his professors. They want to collect lots of samples from the woods. And oh . . . he says we're not to tell anyone about the slime; it must be a total secret.'

Julia discovered that evening that Hal was a good listener. She told him all about the slime and was sure John wouldn't mind – Hal seemed already to be so much part of the family. When she had finished Hal asked lots of questions: he wanted to know about everything not just the slime: the family, their neighbours, the nearest towns. Julia was happy to answer them all and to go on talking to him as long as he liked. She had never felt herself to be so at ease with a stranger before; it was as though they had always been friends.

She told him about Mrs B. and how she fitted into their family. Hal seemed particularly interested in what she, Julia, had to say about Mrs B.'s recent publicity in the local press. She found a copy of the paper and pointed at the large headline. FLYING SAUCER HOVERS OVER WIDOW'S COTTAGE.

'It's nothing like what she told us the morning after!' said Julia. She read part of the article aloud and laughed when she came to the bit where Mrs B. described the heavenly music she had heard when the spaceship had passed overhead.

Hal then asked if they had a 'picture' of the country round about. It took a moment or two for them to work out that he meant a map.

'A map? . . . Is that it?' he asked Julia's mother as Julia went to fetch her school atlas.

'Yes . . . that's right. But I don't think Julia's school atlas will help you much . . . the scale is far too small. I'm sure we've got an Ordinance Survey map of the area here in this drawer. Here it is,' she said, fishing out a badly folded sheet map and spreading it out on the table.

But Julia carefully pointed out to Hal the exact area of England covered by her map. Hal scrutinised both maps closely; every detail from Filkins Wood on the local map to the Falkland Islands in the atlas. He listened intently as Julia read out the names of the places. He followed the courses of rivers with his finger and traced the outlines of oceans.

At that moment two cats came in through the cat flap in the back door. One of them leapt up on to the table and settled down on the Pennines with a paw extending well out into the Irish Sea. The other cat jumped quietly up on to Hal's lap. It stretched up momentarily, nuzzled its nose against his chin and then settled down to purr in comfort.

'Seamus likes you!' said Mrs Garstang.

'It's Finbar, Mum!' Julia corrected her mother and then went on to explain to Hal. Seamus was their own cat; Finbar (as Julia had named him) was a stray. Seamus had vanished for a couple of days but when he returned he had brought with him another black Manx almost identical to himself. It was a mystery where he had come from. Seamus was the only Manx in the vicinity and had come from a litter twenty miles away.

Mrs Garstang suggested that it was time that Julia went up to bed. Hal asked if he might be allowed to take the maps to his room. One of the cats followed him upstairs.

It was strange, thought Julia as she lay in bed thinking about the extraordinary day, how things seemed to be doubling up. Seamus with a twin, Ben with a friend who looked just like him, white violets spreading out through the woods in a way they had never done before. There seemed to be no rhyme or reason for it all. And then there were the orchids. This set her thinking about her conversation with John and she fell asleep dreaming of carpets of yellow stars.

CHAPTER 8
The Sea Bed

'What's this? . . . early morning hydrangea worship?' taunted Ben as he stood at the back door stretching his arms in the warm sunshine, well slept and no longer drained of energy.

Julia and Hal were kneeling close together on the path their heads stuck into the blue-flowered hydrangea bush.

'Can anyone join in? . . . or is it an exclusive religion?' he continued to tease as Julia scrambled hurriedly to her feet.

'What do you mean "early"?' she countered defiantly. 'It's 1.30 in the afternoon you lazy lump . . . we've all been up for hours.'

'I needed the beauty sleep!' said Ben, grinning as he noticed that Julia appeared flustered.

'I was showing Hal our patch of white violets,' she explained. 'We wanted to see if they smelt as sweet as the purple ones at the top of the garden – and they *do* . . . every bit as strong.'

She pushed past him, still slightly embarrassed, and went into the kitchen.

'We talked to John on the phone last night,' she said changing the subject.

Ben's face clouded.

'What did you have to do that for?' he asked crossly. 'You didn't tell him about the sail did you? He'll be furious.'

'It's O.K. . . . Mum talked to him about that and he doesn't mind. He says he'd be happy to go halves with you for a new one . . . and he said you should go out windsurfing again as soon as possible. So as not to lose your nerve.'

Ben's face brightened. At that moment his mother came into the room having overheard their conversation.

'I'm sorry, Ben – I know you wanted to tell John about it but he *did* phone and you were sound asleep,' she said taking no notice of Julia's very pointed stare. 'He also told me that he once got stuck out at sea, too . . . and he never told us. He had to be towed back by a passing power boat. Did he ever tell you about that? I must say I'm quite glad I didn't know . . . I'd have worried and probably never let *you* go windsurfing!'

'Then I'm glad he didn't tell you!' replied Ben.

'He's coming down again in a few days,' Julia interjected.

'Just because of my accident?' Ben sounded a bit put out. 'I'm not a patient in hospital!'

'No . . . O Big Head! You aren't the centre of attraction all the time! He's bringing a couple of professors to look for more of that slime stuff. Apparently it's really interesting . . . a major discovery he called it . . . a mutation of some sort. And we're not to talk to anybody about it.'

'Why not for heaven's sake?'

She shrugged her shoulders.

'Something about not wanting competitors getting their hands on it I think.'

'Competitors? Who'd want the slime anyway?' Ben looked incredulous. And then he added, 'Well I expect there's plenty of it to go round . . . I'm sure I saw some of the stuff yesterday out at sea.'

A call from Ben brought Hal and Julia to the T.V. room.

'They've found something on the sea bed . . . you remember, Julia? The fireball?'

She nodded. 'You didn't see it did you Hal?'

Hal shook his head. 'I wasn't here then.'

'It was about . . .' she began to explain until Ben shushed her up.

'Shut up you two – I want to know what that thing was.' A science correspondent was explaining how a chunk of the fireball had been located on the sea floor. A small submarine had been used: Ben recognised it as the sort normally used for dealing with deep water repairs to oil rig platforms. A piece of film taken by the navy, showed the salvage vessel hauling the object up out of the water. The quality of film was poor. It seemed to have been filmed in the early hours of a cold grey dawn.

With a great clanking of chains and whirring of motors a large curved chunk of what appeared to be blackened metal emerged from the water and hung dripping for some moments before being swung slowly in over the deck. It must have been five or six metres across. Geiger counters checked that it posed no danger: if the object was part of a space craft then the lack of radioactivity suggested that it had not possessed a nuclear engine.

'Funny to think that that's all it is,' said Julia, 'it was so beautiful when it blazed across the sky that night.'

'Belt up and listen!' Ben flung the words at her over his shoulder. She had been talking to Hal and wanted to describe to him what they had seen when standing at the bus stop. It was much more interesting than pictures of a twisted bit of metal dredged up from the bottom of the Atlantic. But now she noticed that Hal wasn't listening to her at all. He was completely absorbed in what was being shown on the screen.

'What *is* it?' muttered Ben to himself.

The Navy had not given very much information when they provided the T.V. networks with the piece of film. The object would be examined by Government scientists, viewers were told, and a report would be issued in due course. If it turned out to be a chunk of an iron asteroid then it would eventually be put on show at the Science Museum in South Kensington for the public to see.

The sports news followed.

'They're hiding something . . . they *must* be,' said Ben passionately. 'Did you notice? They showed us no real close-ups? And did you see how smooth it was on one side when it swung round just before it landed on the deck? It looked like part of a shell from a giant chestnut . . . you know . . . all rough and spiky on the outside and smooth inside. If it was an asteroid it wouldn't have looked like that. I bet there was something *inside* it which they aren't telling us about.'

Hal just listened.

Ben's suspicions were justified, though he wouldn't have the satisfaction of knowing that he was right for some time. The film provided by the navy was already more than a week old. Since then several smaller pieces of the fireball had been salvaged and they confirmed the impression that they were bits of a broken shell or container. Other people noticed the resemblance to the shell segments of an opened chestnut; when the top secret search for the contents of the fireball was put into effect it was given the code name 'Operation Flying Chestnut'.

The tough outer layers of the shell turned out on analysis to be harder than diamond and were covered with markings which suggested that the shell was an artifact made by an advanced intelligence. It was made from materials which baffled the scientists.

The press were kept in the dark about these developments on the grounds that the public might panic if they were to learn the whole truth. What was it that had broken out of the shell at forty thousand feet, long before the disintegrating fragments of the object hit the sea? Had it also disintegrated on entry – or was it coated with some radar-invisible substance like the Stealth bombers of the U.S. air force? And if it had not been burnt up on re-entry then where in its flight around the world had the shell's mysterious cargo been released?

Answering Hal's questions became a full-time occupation for the whole family. He had all the irrepressible eagerness and insistency of a small child who has just discovered the question 'why?'.

The change in him was dramatic. Ben recollected how hesitant Hal had been when he first talked with him. He described to his mother how he had met him and what a solitary and lonely figure he had seemed. As far as they could discover Hal had no friends.

Now he smiled a lot, his hair swept back from his face, and engaged in conversation all the time. He had even been waiting in the kitchen, eager to start talking, when they came down to breakfast on the Monday morning.

It was a school day. Hal would gladly have gone with Julia and Ben, if he had been allowed to, but their mother suggested that he might like to go another time, after she had written a note to the school. And anyway, since she wasn't going to work that day, she relished the opportunity to get to know their unexpected guest a little better. Her children had often had friends to stay but never anybody like Hal. His looks still astonished and troubled her and it was strange the way he immediately fitted in with the family: it was as though he had been with them for years and not just for that weekend. She felt a great urge to protect him and had been moved and upset when Ben had described Hal as a friendless figure on the beach.

There was something childlike about Hal. He had an openness, enthusiasm and innocence which radiated from his face and yet, at the same time, he seemed independent and mature. Which of these characteristics predominated she wondered; but she couldn't decide; and what possible experiences could have led to his having such an unusual character?

After Julia and Ben had run for the school bus and her husband had driven off to work Dorothy Garstang went out into the garden to cut some chives for a salad. Hal followed her up the path and examined everything on the way. What's this? What's that? Why do you grow these? he questioned. He looked at things with a new fresh eye, stopping and staring at plants in the garden which she had taken for granted. She told him the names of every flower and plant she knew and admitted to ignorance when she had to. As they walked back down the garden path she stooped to pull the head off a dandelion.

'Why did you do that?' he queried looking shocked.

'This?' she replied, handing him the head of the flower. 'It's a weed.'

Hal gazed at the tight spray of yellow petals in his hand: an image of the sun. He looked down at the green path of serrated leaves on the path splaying out from a crack between two paving stones; the broken stem of the plucked flower oozing white juice.

'A weed? It's beautiful.'

'We do leave *some* things which we didn't plant . . .' she continued defensively, and pointed towards the hedge where an untidy patch of nettles grew rampantly. '. . . Many people call *those* weeds – they spread terribly fast and they sting; but we leave them to grow there for the red admiral butterflies to lay their eggs on.

'And some things were planted by previous owners . . . that rowan tree for example.' She pointed to the mountain ash growing by the gate. 'There was an old custom amongst the farmers in the north of England to plant rowan trees at the gates to their farms to protect their cattle from witches. In the winter the tree's covered with lovely red berries; the birds adore them.'

'Witches?' queried Hal looking perplexed.

'Witches? You must know about witches. Nobody believes in them these days. Some of them were thought to have the evil eye.'

'The evil eye?' Hal's brow was furrowed.

'Yes . . . they believed that a witch could put a curse on the animals causing a cow's milk to dry up, for example, or a sheep to produce a stillborn lamb. The red-berried rowan tree protected them from the curse.'

'But why do some people want to hurt other people?'

She shrugged.

'Human nature? Far worse things have been done this century than any witch was supposed to have done.'

She saw his cheerful face cloud for the first time.

Mrs B. dropped in half an hour after Ben and Julia returned from school. It wasn't her usual day but she was feeling desperately inquisitive about Hal. When she saw how like Ben he looked, she made the inevitable joke about Dorothy Garstang having children 'what she hadn't let on about'.

She scrutinised Hal while hearing of his hero-ism and gave vent to many an 'ooh!' and an 'aah!'. But she still found it hard to accept that he was merely a chance look-alike of Ben's, albeit a little older, and not a relative – cousin perhaps?

'Must be something in the air!' she joked. 'First, Seamus finds a twin to play with, then Ben gets saved by a look-alike! Whatever next?'

'Be rational, Mrs B . . . there's no connection!' said Ben laughing but feeling irritated that once more people were paying attention to his personal appearance.

'Don't you be so sure, Ben,' she replied sharply. She was fond of the lad but never liked being told that her ideas weren't 'rational' – whatever that was supposed to mean – and particularly by one so young. '*All* things have connections. Life's more mysterious than *you* could have found in *your* short number of years. You mark my words.

'But I was wondering . . .' she continued, her voice suddenly mellowing as she remembered another reason why she had called in on a Monday tea time, 'if you could pop round when you've got a spare minute? Old Armstrong, he finally delivered those logs he'd been promising . . . dumped the lot right at my gate and drove off soon as I'd paid him . . . said he was too busy to stack 'em for me. I was wondering if you'd be kind enough to come down and carry them through to the back for me . . . and stack 'em in my shed?'

Normally Ben would have been happy to be

helpful. But today, although he didn't like to admit it, he felt exhausted again. And he had homework to do. It wasn't much – it would take no more than fifteen minutes if he got on with it – but it hung over the evening like a cloud. He was trying to think of an excuse and mumbling something about being free later in the week, when Hal interrupted him.

'Carry something for you? I'll do it . . . we both will . . . won't we?' He spoke with such unaffected enthusiasm that, surprisingly, all Ben could do was agree. Julia volunteered to help as well.

'Well now!' beamed Mrs B. 'And here's someone who'll earn his keep!' She was fast taking a liking to Hal and her head kept nodding away with approval.

Within fifteen minutes they were ferrying armfuls of logs up Mrs Birtwhistle's front path, through the front door, out the back and into a lean-to shed by the kitchen window.

'Just like little kids!' thought Mrs B. as she listened to their laughter and watched the chunks of bark litter the floor as logs rolled beneath her sideboard in the kitchen and under the old brolly stand in the hall. She decided to ignore the debris along the route – she would clear it up afterwards – and she showered them with thanks, biscuits and lemonade in regular succession.

Hal announced the next day that he wanted to

learn to read English. He was learning to speak the language fast but now he wanted to be able to read it too. Julia had just returned from school on her own: Ben was staying late for a cricket match. She offered to teach Hal immediately.

They retreated to the top of the garden with the day's newspaper and a cup of tea and sat beneath the oldest of the apple trees. Julia lent against the trunk while Hal peered over her shoulder. This was far more fun, thought Julia, than stopping off to have tea with Bessy as she sometimes did.

She had never taught anyone to read before and had no idea how to begin. She had suspected that Hal couldn't read when they had been looking at the maps but hadn't liked to ask him why. Now she pointed with her finger and read some of the headlines and then a full column about the prime minister opening a space-plane factory. Hal listened intently to every word and followed the movement of her finger. Whenever she paused, his eyes quickly scanned the rest of the page.

'There are twenty-six recurring symbols,' he commented after awhile; and then added, 'and some tiny marks which make you pause as you read.'

'Don't you have twenty-six letters in your alphabet?' she asked, giving him an odd look. She wondered if he had been listening to anything she read.

'Go on!' he insisted, ignoring her question. 'I'm beginning to get the hang of it.'

Obediently, Julia read on. Normally nothing would make her read aloud. She loved to be absorbed quietly in a book, but having people listen to her was a pain and an embarrassment. She had the continual fear that she was going to stumble, come across a word she couldn't pronounce or lose the meaning of a sentence by reading with the wrong emphasis and intonation. It was a nightmare. That very day she had had to read aloud in class and she had hated every minute of it, wanting to curl up inside. Some of her friends seemed to love the limelight and always clamoured to read next. Not Julia. She wished she felt differently about it.

Reading with Hal was different. She felt easy in his presence, and not at all awkward about making mistakes; it was as though she had known him all her life like a brother. Or even closer than a brother – she wouldn't willingly read aloud to Ben. He'd be sure to laugh when she got a word wrong and to mock her hesitations.

She read some more headlines.

TERRORISTS PLANT BOMB IN PARIS SUBURB . . . . . . REVOLUTION IN WEST AFRICAN STATE – 54 DEAD . . . . NUCLEAR DISARMAMENT TALKS BREAK DOWN . . . .

Hal's face grew longer and longer.

'What an angry world . . .' he said with a sigh.

'Terrible isn't it?' she agreed. 'And all those people are supposed to be *adults* . . . But the news must be the same in your newspapers?'

Hal made no comment; he was already absorbed in an item at the bottom of the page. Slowly he read it for himself.

DOLPHIN POPULATION IN DECLINE

'What are dolphins?'

'You know,' she said, 'they are mammals that swim in the sea like fish . . . they're intelligent and talk to each other with clicks and whistles . . . you *must* have seen them on television?'

'Well, listen,' he said and then, with very few mistakes but some odd pronunciations, which Julia corrected, Hal read the complete news item to her. A fast decline in the numbers of dolphins in the Pacific had been noted in an ocean-life survey. The article speculated that illegal fishing was a major factor in causing the dwindling numbers. Many dolphins got caught in nets intended for tuna fish: they finished up in tins of cat meat on supermarket shelves.

'How sad,' he commented and Julia agreed; but then she brightened.

'Your reading's fantastic! . . . Go on . . . read something else.'

By the time Julia's mother called from the back door asking what they would like for supper, Hal was reading fast and effectively. If she could pick up new skills as fast as Hal did, Julia thought, she would never have to go to school again.

CHAPTER 9

Julianum

The following day John arrived by car with
two men Julia had never seen before. One of
them, she guessed correctly, had to be John's
professor.

The kitchen seemed over full of people. John
introduced Professor Duckworth to everyone
and then he, larger than life himself, introduced
his colleague as though he were addressing an
audience in a lecture theatre.

'I would like you to meet Professor Harry
Wolf,' he boomed, 'Visiting Professor from
Chicago . . . and one of the *great* micro-
biologists of all time; and I'm proud to say, a
member of my department for the time being.
I brought Harry along because I value his opinion, I can trust him with a secret . . . unlike
many of my colleagues . . . blabbermouths all
of them. You know . . . we're on to something really quite remarkable here? A *unique*
organism. A solution to the world's pollution

problems . . . a greater discovery even than the invention of drains! It'll save industry millions of pounds . . . billions . . . you've no idea the impact it'll have on the economy! And it'll mean clean rivers, safe unpolluted beaches, fresh living lakes.'

It was quite a speech. He paused for a moment's thought and then, talking quietly for a change, added wistfully, with a glance at John, 'You know . . . there could even be a Nobel prize in it somewhere!'

'It sure is the case,' affirmed the American, as he shook hands energetically with everyone in the room. 'That's quite some plant you've discovered.'

Apart from being loud, the two professors were physically large and intimidating and they made the room seem unusually small.

Hal broke the silence, which followed their introductions, by introducing himself to John.

'Hello! I'm Hal,' he said shaking his hand. And then he added, 'I hope you don't mind?'

'Don't mind?' queried John. It was extraordinary, he was thinking, to meet a stranger who looked so much like an older version of his brother.

'Your clothes – I'm wearing them.'

'Oh . . . I see . . . I didn't recognise them! . . . No! That's fine. I'm glad they fit.'

'You two not related?' asked the American.

Dorothy Garstang explained how Hal had

come to them so dramatically, stepping out of the sea into their family life.

'Rare to find two people looking so much alike who aren't related,' commented the American looking puzzled. He scrutinized Ben and then Hal in turn. 'There must be some ancestral genes in common. Maybe you should probe way back through your families to see if there's any distant connection. Could be interesting for you.'

John had turned to speak to his professor. It seemed odd to have the man standing here, a guest in his own home.

'Er . . . Bill,' he began and then immediately regretted it. He was quite used to calling Harry Wolf 'Harry' but never Professor Duckworth 'Bill'. He raced on to cover his confusion. 'How about going up to Filkins Wood straight away? Mum says she'll make supper for everyone so you needn't worry about getting back to your hotel.'

Professor Duckworth appeared delighted with the suggestion, and to John's relief seemed not to have registered the way he had addressed him.

'Wonderful, wonderful, that's very kind of you, Mrs Garstang,' he said with the loud air of someone used to having things done for him. 'Shall we all go? Let's make an expedition of it! Come on! John, you lead the way!'

He ought to have been a general in the army, Julia thought to herself.

★

Three hours later the kitchen once more exploded with noise and Dorothy Garstang wondered if all professors talked with such loud voices.

'Any success?' she asked.

John shook his head. 'Not if you mean did we find any slime – there wasn't even a slither of it to be found anywhere. And we checked in all the likely places. But we did collect a lot of samples. We got pots of soil; and masses of scrapings from rocks and tree trunks. And some of the water from the pool. And Hal was fantastic in helping us!' John looked around the room to make sure that Hal would hear his praise. 'He stripped off and swam out to the middle of the pool to lower a nifty little device of Harry's on a piece of string. We've got a sample now from really deep down.'

John's mother beamed at Hal proudly. 'We already knew he was a good swimmer!' she said.

'But we never found any sign of those five orchids or whatever they were that John replanted,' said Professor Duckworth. 'I'm positive they were another form this remarkable plant can take. Are you sure they were *exactly* like orchids?' he asked, turning to John.

'I could kick myself for not examining them more closely.'

'Quite so!' boomed the professor back at him. 'Very unscientific of you not to have looked closer!'

'But at the time I had no reason to suspect . . .' John dried up as he felt the professor's withering stare bear down on him. He knew when it was useless to argue.

Conversation at supper returned inevitably to the subject of the disappearing slime. Only Ben, his mother noticed, had very little to say. She blamed herself. When they had been ready to sit down for the meal she had asked Ben to fetch some chairs from the next room, but then noticing that Hal was already doing so, had accused her son of not showing enough initiative – unlike Hal. The harm was done.

For the first time it occurred to her that Ben might find it a strain having Hal to stay with them. Julia and Hal were as thick as thieves, and that she supposed might be part of the problem. In fact Julia had hardly paid any attention to her brother for the past few days; not even to argue. Not that Hal was anything but charming and certainly not competitive but he had stolen the limelight. And because of his courage in the storm Ben was in the unenviable position of being the one who'd suffered and been saved. He couldn't even boast about the adventure any more with Hal still on the scene. She knew she had to have a good talk with him.

'The trouble is . . . that specimen at the lab is the only one we've got . . .' the American was saying, 'unless those soil samples we've collected contain any spores.'

'Which means,' interrupted Professor Duckworth looking at Julia, 'that if it hadn't been for *you*, young girl . . . we wouldn't have any of it. And what we would have missed!' He beamed at her with unqualified gratitude and then adopting his stentorian lecturing voice proclaimed with a dramatic flourish of his arm:

'I am therefore happy to announce – for the first time in public – that this organism has been named *Filkinsiense silvestri Julianum.*'

'Julia! A slime named after you! Wait till I tell your friends at school!' taunted Ben.

Hal clapped and looked so genuinely pleased that Julia could have hugged him.

'You'll get your name in the biology books!' said her dad with pride.

'Not just the biology books,' said Professor Duckworth 'newspapers, economic text books; books on ecology, the environment, green issues . . . the lot. What we've got here is green gold!'

Julia herself looked pleased but sheepish.

'So what became of all the slime in the pool?' asked Dorothy Garstang. 'Did it all turn into slugs and little yellow flowers do you think? Or did it all get washed down to the sea?'

'There was no sign of anything unusual in the woods at all,' said the American, 'except for that wonderful display of the white variety of *viola aromata* the white violet – I've never seen such a fantastic sight in a woodland before. You do have some very lovely countryside around here!' Then he added, returning to the subject of the slime, 'But I don't think it would have all got washed down to the sea . . . there's too many places for it to get caught up on, on the way.'

'But some did . . . Ben saw it didn't you?' Julia interjected.

Ben nodded and then when pressed told briefly that he thought he had seen some when he'd been windsurfing.

'The important thing,' said Professor Duckworth, 'is that *we've* got some. It's a rare, unique, mutation and we can *use* it.'

'Mutation?' asked Julia.

The Professor fished an envelope out of his pocket and quickly drew a diagram.

'It's like this . . . all living things, animals and plants, are made up of cells, millions of them. Look here's a cell, this wobbly shape looking like a floppy balloon. But each cell is so small you can hardly see it with the naked eye.'

Now he scribbled a large black dot in the middle of his drawing.

'If you examined it through a microscope you'd see that each cell has a nucleus at the centre like this. The nucleus is the bundle of information which contains a complete description of the animal . . . in the language of chemistry of course.

104

'A *mutation* is when a bit of that information gets changed. (It may have got copied wrong or damaged). When the information changes then the shape of the whole creature changes in some way. Or to be more accurate, the shape of that creature's offspring. If it's a short-haired dog for instance, the mutation might lead to the dog giving birth to long-haired pups.'

'Or in a bad case to a pup with two heads,' contributed the American.

Julia grimaced.

'But they aren't all bad, these mutations,' he added hastily. 'Every living thing you see in this world is the result of mutations. All the rich diversity of the jungles. Every animal in the zoo. And people too. We all have to be grateful for mutations . . . without them none of us would be here. That's how life evolved on Earth.'

'Is that chemistry in the nucleus the DNA stuff John is always talking about?' Julia asked tentatively.

'That's it. Exactly!' beamed the Professor. He leaned across the table and took hold of her hand. 'And do you realize, the DNA in every single cell in your body contains all the information needed to construct an exact living copy of *you*? Just one cell from the skin on the back of your hand would be enough – if we had the technology – to make another Julia: a clone. We can already do it with plants; some day, in the very distant future, we may be able to do it with people. How about some identical sisters?'

'What a thought! One's quite enough!' Ben sounded aghast.

'Ben! Shut up!' Julia replied sharply. 'It's interesting.'

'But there is one very significant oddity about JULIANUM,' said the Professor releasing Julia's hand. 'We've found that each cell has *three* nuclei.' He scribbled two more dark blobs in the middle of the sketch he had drawn on the back of the envelope. 'And they are *packed* with DNA.'

'It's a mystery, Bill,' said his colleague nodding slowly.

Hal, who had been silent for some time, absorbing all that was being said, got up from where he sat and walked round to the professor. Leaning over his shoulder he pointed to one of the nuclei in the diagram.

'Animals?' he suggested. Then he pointed at the next nucleus and said, 'Plants.' The third nucleus caused him to hesitate for a moment before saying, 'Other types of creature.'

The American let out a great burst of laughter. 'Hey . . . that's quite some theory! You should go in for science-fiction writing, young man . . . with an imagination like that! But no, seriously . . . there's no way that one cell could carry the DNA of different types of creature. Evolution would never create something so bizarre.'

'Just an idea.' Hal shrugged and a smile briefly

flitted across his face. Then, quietly excusing himself, he left the room.

'I bet he's gone to read the encyclopaedias,' whispered Julia, when he was out of earshot. 'He's fantastically clever! He spoke very little English last weekend and listen to him now! . . . And last night he learnt to read English in just an hour. I read him the newspaper and he picked it up just like that!' She flicked her fingers. 'Then he asked me what else we had to read and I showed him our books. He picked out an encyclopaedia and plunged straight into an article on . . . I think it was astro . . . astrophysics.'

'Is that so?' Harry Wolf looked interested. 'Geniuses have always fascinated me . . . their brain power and their originality. But, you know, they can be lonely people – isolated from the rest of us.'

'Hal was certainly a loner until last week,' Ben agreed. 'But now he seems to talk all the time . . . it's quite exhausting. And he sucks up information like a vacuum cleaner.'

Just before the two professors left to go to their hotel for the night, Julia wanted to ask one last question. She was catching the enquiring habit from Hal. How did all the separate cells of the slime know how and when to get themselves together when they were due to become a slug? What organised them? How did they know, without having brains, how to arrange themselves? And how could a slug turn itself into a miniature garden of flowers as *Julianum* had done or into a single flower as with the slime moulds John was researching for his thesis?

'Chemical switch,' replied Professor Duckworth curtly, putting on his coat as he spoke. He had had enough for the evening and he wanted to go to bed. 'A chemical you won't have heard of,' he added to forestall any further questions.

Julia was duly silenced.

Harry Wolf thought she deserved a better answer. 'I prefer the account that blames it on a wicked witch,' he said. 'Have you read any of that great Elizabethan writer of yours – Spenser? In his old tale *The Faerie Queen* there's a cruel witch called Acrasia. She's the traditional wicked witch you hear of in so many fairy tales – attractive but cold; powerful and evil. In *The Faerie Queen* she attracts men; but then, when she has them in her power, she turns them into beasts . . . and they lose their freedom for ever. It's *that* power to change something into something else which led chemists to name a very remarkable chemical after Acrasia. They called it acrasin. And that's the stuff Bill was talking about. It's acrasin which switches on the cells in slime moulds and makes them form up in regimental order as a slug; and it's acrasin which later turns the whole thing into a fruiting body like a flower.'

'So is there something deep down in Filkins

Pool which switched on all the slime and made it turn into something else?' asked Julia.

'There you have us guessing!' he answered with a grin. 'But look, seeing you're so interested and you have got a sort of proprietorial claim on *Julianum*, why don't you come back to the university with us tomorrow night? Spend a long weekend with your brother John and have a look at some of our experiments? See the miniature *Julianum* garden for yourself.' He then added in a persuasive sort of tone, looking at Julia's mother, 'It could even give a boost to your science studies at school!'

CHAPTER 10

A Black Limousine

It was the first time that Julia had been to stay with John. She looked at the buildings beyond the car park: they must be part of the university she supposed but it all seemed much more spread-out and modern than she had expected. She stood, sports bag in hand, surveying the scene while John and the two professors unloaded the rest of the luggage from the car.

A thick-set figure at the far end of the car park, striding purposefully towards them, caught her eye. Julia was the first to notice him. Even at that distance she could sense he was in a rage. She tapped her brother on the arm as he handed a case full of specimen bottles to Harry Wolf from the boot of the car.

'Who's that man? I think he wants something.'

John looked up. 'Oh! What's got into *him*?'

Julia looked at her brother enquiringly.

'Its the university bursar, Brigadier Bagshot-Blunt . . . and it looks rather as though he is in one of his bristling military rages!'

The last person Professor Duckworth wanted to get involved with, just at that moment, was the bursar. He was impatient to get to his equipment and examine the rather unhopeful-looking collection of samples from in and around Filkins woods; and to check the small quantity of *Julianum* which they had left in the laboratory. He hoped that no one had tampered with it.

'Professor Duckworth!' bawled the bursar as he zig-zagged between the parked vehicles.

'Your attitude to dangerous experiments is quite unacceptably cavalier!' he barked as soon as he judged himself to be within certain ear-shot. 'You're an unmitigated disaster, sir . . . an irresponsible madman! And where have you been? I've had my assistants waste their time searching every café, pub and restaurant in town. You know very well that hazardous experiments should be supervised at *all* times. Yet you go off without a word to anyone. Well, sir?'

The barrage of accusations left the Professor temporarily reeling. 'I . . . er . . . I'm sure everything is in proper order,' he replied rather lamely.

'In . . . proper . . . order?' Brigadier Bagshot-Blunt articulated the words slowly with the confidence of a man who thinks he has the upper hand. The bursar worshipped precise organisation and neatness: everything in his life had a proper place; the items on his desk always gave the impression of having been laid out with a ruler; and his day was governed by a clock with an accurate second hand.

'In proper order?' he asked again with heavy sarcasm. 'I think you had better come with me,' said the bursar. And with that, he turned sharply on his heel and marched briskly out of the car park.

They shrugged their shoulders at each other and followed quietly.

'I expect somebody's blocked a fire exit with bits of equipment – or used the wrong waste bin for his litmus paper and chewing gum!' suggested John in a low voice.

'In Chicago we had a famous bursar,' said Professor Wolf, 'who once shot a student who was in college a minute after the place should have been locked up for the night . . . got him in the leg and then charged him with trespass!'

They turned the corner around the back of the library buildings and then abruptly stopped. Julia gasped and moved closer to her brother. A group of firemen stood in their way gripping a hosepipe. They were playing a jet of water down on to the path which led to the microbiology laboratories.

'We've managed to hold it back on this side, sir,' one of the firemen said to the bursar.

A tide of green slime covered the quad. It heaped up into a roll where the pressure of water held it back. The three-storied block which housed the laboratories was dripping, oozing, glistening with strands and sheets of slime; tentacles of it crept up over the roof while rivers of green cascaded out of the windows.

'Just like the Everglades,' whispered Professor Wolf with awe.

The slime extended well beyond the laboratory block. A thin layer covered the paving in the quad and still more hung in curtains from the large copper beech tree that filled the space between the labs and the administration building – the building which housed the bursar's office.

'Well?' asked the bursar accusingly. He let the question hang in the air.

'Magnificent! Fascinating!' said the professor. 'What a life-force!' he went on, completely ignoring the bursar. If only, he thought to himself, he could convince the relevant authorities that *he*, in *his* laboratory, had developed this pollution-eating slime, this gourmet of toxic waste, then fame and fortune would come rolling in. It was now even more urgent that he register the patent with the patent office, before *Julianum* became common property.

'Well?' repeated Brigadier Bagshot-Blunt, his fury coming back to the boil. 'I'm told that this is one of *your* little creations!'

Professor Duckworth nodded with proprietorial pleasure. His American colleague put a hand on his shoulder.

'That surely is some slime, Bill!' he said with admiration. We've got nothing like that in the States – even the Everglades can't match it!'

The bursar's face clouded. 'Do you know what it's going to cost to clear this mess up?' he thundered.

'I told you it had something to do with waste disposal,' whispered John to his sister. 'I just got the scale wrong!' He surveyed the vast quantities of slime with astonishment. 'Is this what it was like when you first saw it with Ben?'

Julia nodded. 'Except it wasn't climbing up over everything like this – it was just clogging the pool. But I can't believe that all *that* has grown from what was left in the bottle behind the hydrangea bush. It's fantastic!'

The bursar briefly shot her a hostile glance before returning his attention to Professor Duckworth.

'Turn the damned stuff off!' he roared.

'Turn it off?' repeated Professor Duckworth.

'Yes – switch it off before it gets to the library or invades the bursary!'

Professor Duckworth sighed. 'I'm afraid that that may not be so easy. You see I don't know yet what switched it on.'

'You must understand, Bursar . . .' Harry Wolf began to explain gently, taking the bursar by the arm, 'a wicked witch has been at work, and until we find her chemical code there's not very much we can do. You see . . .'

114

The bursar pulled away from him. He was beginning to go a deep shade of purple. 'Sir – you're insane! . . . You don't live in the real world . . . Heaven preserve me from mad academics.' Then turning to Professor Duckworth he fired his final barrage. 'And you, sir . . . get this mess under control immediately or I foresee your departmental allowance going down the drain for the next several years.' With that he strode off to the bursary, carefully skirting the slime, leaving the firemen to keep the green tide in check.

'Oh dear,' groaned the professor. 'I do wish that man would remember that this is a research establishment and not an accountant's office.'

'Well, Governor?' One of the firemen turned to him. 'You're King Canute . . . so what are the orders?'

Fifteen minutes later the four of them, in white coats and wellingtons, stood in the doorway of the laboratory.

'Nice decor you have here, Professor!' quipped Professor Wolf. 'It might catch on!'

The room had been transformed into a green grotto: skeins of protoplasm hung from the ceiling and completely covered the walls. Everything was festooned with the stuff; filing cabinets, stools, benches, basins, bottles, bunsen burners: nothing had escaped the growing green carpet.

They sniffed. There was a strong smell of mushrooms and a faint whiff of gas.

Professor Duckworth brushed his arm across one of the bench tops to clear its surface. 'Blast!' he swore. 'It's taken a liking to the new acid resistant worksurfaces we had fitted. The bursar will be furious. They've only been in place for six months – and the old skinflint complained about the expense then!'

John was sniffing the air again. 'That *is* gas isn't it?' With a gloved hand he cleared a mound of slime from where he guessed a gas tap should be.

'Hey! . . . look at this!' he exclaimed. He beckoned urgently.

The gas tap had been totally dissolved – or consumed. The slime had formed a solid plug which had all but sealed off the exposed gas pipe. Quick investigation – or quick as could be; moving round the lab was a precarious matter – revealed that the same thing had happened to all twenty gas taps in the laboratory. A similar fate had overcome the water taps in the basins; yet despite the great water pressure only the slightest trickle issued from the exposed pipes.

'Extraordinary!' Harry Wolf pondered a moment; then his face lit up.

'Know what?' he asked excitedly '*Julianum* doesn't only have a taste for your acid resistant bench tops or for toxic pollutants – it's drinking the water and breathing the gas –

116

water and methane – H_2O and CH_4 – two of the basic and most common molecules in the universe. That's why it has spread so rapidly.'

'Julia – quickly!' Professor Duckworth commanded. 'Go tell that fireman to get the gas and water turned off pronto! My God think of the next gas bill! Old Bagshot-Blunt will go up in smoke!' He chuckled involuntarily.

By early afternoon the scene had been transformed. Once the gas and water had been turned off, the slime seemed to lose some of its flourishing vitality. Firemen found it easier now to hose down the pathways, walls and steps. Anyone who watched closely, however, would have seen what was really happening. The protoplasm was sinking silently into the soil around the copper beech tree; where there were drains it quietly slithered away.

Television coverage of this quite extraordinary event, much to Professor Duckworth's relief, was very poor. He didn't want the world's attention drawn to *Julianum* before he was ready to make a statement to the scientific community. His relief however was shortlived. A girlfriend of John's, a photography student called Tasha, had been on campus early that morning and had taken some stunning pictures of the slime erupting from the laboratories. It was a scoop and she made a lot of money from selling the pictures to the press. The best of them were faxed around the world and appeared in the next morning's papers.

SLIME SHOCK: STUDENT RAG OR RUN-AWAY EXPERIMENT? ran the headlines in one paper. Others were less serious carrying banner headlines such as RISING DAMP ON CAMPUS? or EVERGLADES COME TO BRITAIN!; and ROT SETS IN AT TOP UNIVERSITY! More cautious papers were content with simpler headlines such as MYSTERY SLIME. Perhaps the most alarming was SECRET BIOLOGICAL WARFARE EXPERIMENT BACKFIRES.

The appearance of a long black limousine finally brought to an end Professor Duckworth's dreams of a Nobel Prize.

Four dark-suited men got out, looked briefly at the biochemistry buildings, which still showed signs of their recent weird envelopment, and after a brief consultation entered the administration building.

The two professors and John were summoned to an empty office and discovered that the men were from the Ministry of Defence. The senior of the four men took the seat behind the large desk. He had no time to waste.

'Well, Professor, it seems you have got something in your laboratory which has got just a little out of hand,' he said, speaking with deliberate understatement. 'Perhaps you would like to tell us about it?'

The professor bridled. He was unused to being cross-examined like this, as though he were a junior employee.

'What right?' he snapped, but was immediately interrupted.

'I'm sorry, Professor . . . to pry into your work like this.' the man behind the desk said firmly, 'but we think the matter is of grave urgency . . . possibly a matter of national security.'

'National security? That's absurd!' The professor was affronted.

There was a moment's silence while no one spoke. The interview had not started well.

'Now look here,' the man leant forward hoping to get the discussion off to a better start. 'Let me do a little explaining . . . warfare isn't what it used to be . . . you know, when armies came out into the open and bashed away at each other until a victor emerged. Not a *bit* of it . . . today's wars are sneaky and underhand . . . urban guerrillas . . . bombs in market places . . . deaths of innocent civilians . . . discreet assassinations. You read about it in the papers all the time. But now we've reached a new stage and it's the worst of all.'

'Go on,' said Professor Duckworth frostily.

'Nowadays the art is to wage war without your enemy even knowing. All you have to do is to make it look like a natural accident. We've got good reason to believe that there are powers in the world, who have invested billions of pounds in researching just how such accidents could be engineered and directed. Defeat would follow without a shot being fired. It used to be called sabotage but on the scale we're discussing now, it's war we're talking about.'

He leant forward and fixed Professor Duckworth with a penetrating stare.

'Now perhaps you see why we are interested in an apparent uncontrolled eruption of . . . um . . . protoplasm from your laboratory?'

The Professor realised now that there was no point in protesting any more and so he told them all that he knew about JULIANUM. He explained that the organism had not been created in his lab but that he had plans to develop its fantastic potential as a biological weapon against pollution. John filled in the details of its discovery.

'So let's recap.' The man behind the desk said, looking serious. He spread out the stack of photos they had picked up that morning from the News Photo Library. John reflected with pleasure what a very good photographer his friend Tasha was becoming.

'All this protoplasm we see here,' the man continued, 'grew in a few hours from what was originally no more than a jugful left behind a hydrangea bush in the north of England . . . a sample which you say your sister (he nodded at John) collected from a local pond in a wood? And from what you say, Professor it thrives dramatically . . . as we can all see . . . on natural gas and water.'

Professor Duckworth inclined his head in agreement.

'My God!' The man sat back in his chair and spread his hands out for effect. 'Why are you scientists so naive? Just think what would happen if this stuff should get into the North Sea! It could finish off the gas industry and the oil too. Our economy would be ruined in a matter of weeks – or even days. We'd be a sitting target for any enemy who wanted to move in.'

There was silence.

The man from the ministry turned and spoke to one of his colleagues.

'Get on to the minister of defence immediately. He'll get clearance from the prime minister.' He turned to Professor Duckworth. 'I'm sorry, Professor but we must take over your department in the interests of national security. And we're going to call in the army. You say you've collected samples from those woods and the pool. I'm afraid we can't wait for you to analyse them. If any of that *Julianum* stuff is still there it must be killed off at all costs.'

CHAPTER 11

Agent Orange

Ben felt irritated with himself for feeling so irritable. There was no logic to it. He had no reason to dislike Hal or to hold anything against him, in fact he owed him gratitude and admiration; but he didn't want to give it. Instead he felt thoroughly put out. He couldn't boast to anyone about his dangerous adventure in the storm as Hal's role had been even more dramatic. And he was fed up with people saying how alike they looked. So what? They were totally different characters. But Hal was so darned clever; much cleverer than he was, quick at everything, with a brain as fast as a computer. 'Genius' was the word John's friends had used.

Then there was Julia; she was devoted to Hal as though he was some great star – or a super-perfect brother. She'd do anything for him. She had almost decided not to go to visit John's university, just because Hal was staying. He didn't really mind being ignored by his sister,

122

he kept telling himself (why should he want her attention anyway?), and yet it had started to aggravate him. The word jealousy never entered his head.

He became silent and sullen. When he thought about it, he felt as though he had lost something; and it was Hal's fault. It was almost as though he had been replaced in the family by a more successful version of himself. Normally, he was just straightforwardly happy and unquestioning about life; a bit full of himself, perhaps: Julia sometimes called him a Big Head and he didn't mind, taking it as sort of compliment. But now his confidence had been toppled and he felt depressed about himself: it was rather like falling off the surfboard when he felt tired – it would take a bit of an effort to pull himself up again.

It was Hal who finally made things easier. On Friday night Ben's mother suggested that he should spend some time with Hal – now that Julia wasn't there to talk to him – play a game, talk, anything; just show him a bit of friendliness, she said. At first he protested that he had a lot of homework to do – which he hadn't – and then, with an ungracious sigh, he agreed.

They played chess, a game at which Ben reckoned he was moderately good, but Ben won the first two games and then Hal made mince meat of him – and Hal rarely had to think for more than a few seconds before making a move.

Hal was very competitive; but it was in a non-crowing sort of way and it was hard to resent his cleverness. Ben felt his animosity starting to melt away. In the concentration of the play he forgot his self-regarding, inward-looking, feelings and when, later that night, Hal challenged his father to a match he found himself taking Hal's side, willing him to win and beaming with delight when he did. He even teased his father about not being a good sport when he retired gruffly after his third rapid defeat.

When his mother suggested that he take Hal windsurfing the next day, Saturday, it suddenly seemed a great idea.

Teaching Hal to windsurf was rather like teaching him to play chess: he improved as you watched, falling in a few times until he got the hang of it and then flowing with the sea and the wind like a professional. He was a natural, his movements always in harmony with the board, never awkward. Ben marvelled at him with real admiration and shared his exuberance. He also forgot any lingering fear he might have had about sailing well away from the land. By Saturday afternoon the two of them were far out towards the horizon cutting the waves at angles to see who could get their surf boards to jump the highest.

Dorothy Garstang took the boys windsurfing

again on Sunday morning. She parked the car at the top of the beach and watched them for a while, proud of their skill. It looked so easy and such fun. Someday, she promised herself, she would hire a board and take lessons – but perhaps not when the family were around.

They had been windsurfing for about an hour when two large power boats packed with soldiers sped down the coast. Ben and Hal gripped their sailbars tightly as the boats roared by smashing through the waves.

'Must be an exercise,' Ben shouted.

The power boats left widening curves of creaming wake behind them as they swung in towards the coast. Hal and Ben tacked slowly in that direction: they could see men, leaping out on to the shore, at the foot of the cliffs where Filkins Beck tumbled down to the sea. While they were watching, four enormous Chinook helicopters appeared from further down the coast: great sausage-shaped machines each with twin engines and two sets of blades on top. They flew in file. When abreast of the cliffs, where the power boats had landed, they turned inland. One landed in a field that skirted the top of the cliffs: almost immediately dozens of soldiers emptied out of it and fanned out in all directions. The remaining three flew on a couple of miles, circled noisily and then settled in the hay fields in the vicinity of Filkins Wood. By now there were soldiers swarming up the cliffs from the shore like an army of meticulous ants.

'I wonder what they are doing?' shouted Ben. 'Funny place for a military exercise. Looks like fun! Maybe I'll join the army! Come on, let's get closer.'

Hal remained silent.

As they got closer they began to make out more details of the operation. The soldiers who were left on the shore had divided into two groups, one moving off to the left and the other to the right. They wore large back packs and carried long rods which, at first sight, Ben had thought were metal detectors.

'They're spraying,' Hal called across to him.

'Spraying? What for?'

'To kill.'

Ben came alongside Hal and then slowly let his sail down into the water and sat astride the board. They were close into shore by now and could hear the soldiers shouting to each other. It seemed a very different place from the day of the storm, Ben thought to himself. He shuddered at the memory of the grey pounding waves, the driving rain and the ragged rocks.

'To kill? But those rock pools are full of rare things. John did a survey of them once as part of his degree . . . crabs, anemones and several protected species. They can't do that – it's wicked and why should they want to anyway?'

At that moment a loud-hailer boomed across

126

the waves from the shore: 'Hallo there! Sorry! No landing here. This is a Ministry of Defence warning. No landing. I repeat, no landing. Please make your way further up the coast. Thank you.'

Road blocks were set up on every route into the area and several square miles of countryside were cordoned off. No one was allowed to enter it and no one was allowed to drive through. Local residents could only come and go with permission and with an elaborate spraying of feet and of vehicles. It was even debated whether they should be evacuated totally; finally it was decided that less fuss would be made if they were allowed to stay.

The army was having a lovely time. A rare opportunity for real emergency manoeuvres had presented itself. More men, more helicopters and more tanks had been deployed than were strictly necessary. It was a chance, a top general had argued, not to be missed. An army in peace time could get weary and flabby with boredom. 'Operation De-scum' was good for the men.

Soldiers roamed the countryside in their all-in-one protective suits, masked helmets and back packs which looked like the sort of apparel worn when dealing with radiation leaks at a power station. They sprayed wherever they went; hedgerows, ditches, puddles, banks and undergrowth – everything got the treatment.

A large contingent made their way up Filkins Beck from the sea spraying as they went. They penetrated every nook and cranny in the rocks about the stream with their killing mist. The woodland floor around Filkins Pool got special attention: tree trunks, rocks, patches of bracken, clusters of wood anemones, white violets: everything was drenched in a fine mist of lethal fungicide and herbicide. The heavily suited soldiers covered the area several times just to be sure that nowhere had been overlooked. Then three large cannisters of poison were dropped into Filkins Pool itself. They were designed to release their contents slowly: minute quantities of the chemicals they contained were guaranteed to kill anything.

'Operation De-scum' was put into effect with a vengeance.

Residents within the cordoned-off zone were bemused and bewildered. The blockade of their countryside had come out of the blue without explanation or apology. Only after the event were they told anything. The Garstangs knew a little more than most but not much. Julia had related the story of *Julianum's* rapid eruption out of the university and its final control; and she had told them about the secret meeting Professor Duckworth and John had been summoned to by the mysterious men from the ministry. John told her that it had all become top secret and it would be easier if she left for home first thing on the Sunday morning. The Ministry of Defence took a serious view of the slime, he explained to her, and were treating it as an act of industrial sabotage – though why anyone wanting to undermine the economy would begin with Filkins Pool she could not fathom.

It fell to the local policeman to try to explain to some of the older inhabitants of the area what was happening. He called on Mrs Birtwhistle about tea time.

Indignant and upset she made her way straight round to the Garstangs'. But not before having her wellingtons sprayed with some evil-smelling disinfectant by two cheeky young soldiers on duty in her lane.

Mrs B. had been at the Garstangs' for about half an hour when the bell rang. Two figures with heavy cylinders on their backs and dressed as though they had stepped right out of a space invaders film were at the back door. One of them raised the mask on his helmet when Julia, with her mother behind her, opened the door.

'Sorry to inconvenience you,' he said. 'We've had orders to spray all your drains, along the sides of your paths and particularly around this hydrangea here.' He paused and looked at the large bush covered in heavy-headed blue flowers. Some of the blooms hung right down to the ground where their blueness seemed even brighter against the carpet of white violets.

'I'm sorry about this,' he repeated. 'But we have to take precautions.'

They could tell from his voice that the bush would die.

'You better shut the back door and fasten all your windows securely so we can get on with it. It's powerful stuff this spray.'

Julia and her mother were speechless. They knew there was no point in arguing and in a way that made it worse. They wanted to protest loudly; but they remained dumb.

'Oh! by the way,' the soldier added as they were about to shut the door. 'Do you know who lives in the cottage just down the road? We've just been there and no one was in.'

'Mrs Birtwhistle . . .' Julia began but the man was clearly in a hurry to get on with carrying out his orders.

'If you see her,' he continued holding up his mask just long enough to finish what he had to say, 'tell her we had to spray half her front garden. A ditch runs along the side of her hedge and we've orders to spray five metres to each side of all ditches and drains.' He pulled the visor down over his face and all possible communication came to an end.

They shut the door and turned to see Mrs B. pale-faced and looking as though all the wind had been knocked out of her.

'All my Michaelmas Daisies,' she murmured. 'Purple and blue and mauve heads they have . . .

beautiful ones. My husband planted them twenty years ago and every autumn they flower right as rain . . .'

Julia noticed Hal standing silently by the door. A dark cloud seemed to have settled across his face. She had never seen him look angry before.

On Monday morning the school bus was only allowed to come as far as the check point half a mile back down the road from the Garstangs' house. Ben and Julia set off to walk in their wellingtons. As they arrived at the barricade ready to have their boots sprayed with disinfectant a large car drew up. They recognised the occupant as he got out; his picture was often in the paper. It was the local M.P.

There were several military men standing around as well as the guards on duty at the road block. One of them was the commander of the unit. He had been waiting for the M.P. to arrive.

'Agent Orange,' explained the commander. 'We left it till last – once the men had done the ground work we could have a go at the tree tops.'

'Agent Orange?' the M.P. was appalled. 'Agent Orange? the Americans used that in Vietnam to defoliate the trees. It only takes minute quantities to produce cancers in people. Who the hell authorised it?'

'Oh, we cleared the woods, sir. There's no one in there at the moment. I'm afraid it has to be done Sir . . . no alternative. Did you see the pictures of that stuff at the university when it got out of hand . . . how it spread right up over that tree? . . . we're spraying a belt a hundred metres to each side of the stream . . . that should kill it off.'

Although unaware of it, the M.P. was not the only one that morning to be angry with this military turn of events. 'Operation De-scum' had been put into effect so fast that there had been no proper liaison with other branches of the Intelligence Services. Another unit, responsible for tracing the contents of the fireball which had disintegrated in the Atlantic, had kept their own research so secret that they had been omitted from the list of those to be alerted about the use of Agent Orange. 'Operation Flying Chestnut' had made good progress: search for the lost contents of the fireball had narrowed the focus down to the north of England. Several sightings of something strange in the sky over the Irish sea had alerted them; Mrs Birtwhistle's report to the local police had clinched the matter. But now just as they were poised on the verge of success and about to uncover the mystery of what it was that had landed from space, the army had got there before them and sprayed the whole area with lethal poisons. Furious meetings behind closed doors in Whitehall followed. Accusations were made of right hands not knowing what left hands were doing: resignations were demanded.

The hedgerows and ditches soon began to wilt and die. Not the natural death of autumn with its soft tints and its crisp leaves but a dank and ugly death a grey and shrivelled discolouration of the countryside. Within a few days the disfigured landscape would look like winter. The trees that shaded the muddy lane, turning the track in summer into an enchanted green tunnel, would become skeletons against the sky. The army had been liberal with its use of Agent Orange. Filkins Wood suffered the worst devastation; but then there was no one to see it because no one was allowed into Filkins Wood.

CHAPTER 12

Blue Cornflowers

While death was being sprayed in a long scar across the summer countryside in one part of England a strange spring was taking hold in another.

John was one of the first to notice. What he saw perplexed him and he wondered if he could trust his memory but then it became quite clear that something very odd was happening. The lawn at the back of the laboratories was normally kept cut and rolled like a bowling green. The bursar with his obsession for order and tidiness liked the lawn to have neat sharp edges and not a daisy in sight. He had even wanted to put up 'Keep off the Grass' notices but his intentions had been frustrated by an angry deputation of students who had got wind of his plans.

The lawn had been transformed overnight into a rich and wild meadow. Ox-eye daisies, purple clover, cowslips and crowsfoot-trefoil grew in profusion through the thick swathes of grass:

and many more varieties besides. It looked well established and natural as though it had always been like that; which was why John wondered at first if his memory was playing tricks on him.

It was when he saw some discreet clumps of white violets, which had appeared as if from nowhere, growing at the foot of the great copper beech tree in the quad, that an idea began to dawn. It seemed impossible, unreal. It didn't make sense but it had to be tested. He had to check.

A blue cornflower was picked from the meadow and a white violet from beside the path. They were examined carefully beneath a powerful microscope. His hunch had been right: *Julianum* both of them. The revelation left the researchers in the laboratory speechless. Why had they been so blind? Why had they clung to their assumption that JULIANUM was just a mutation of some rare form of slime mould with exotic flowers and a taste for pollution? And it certainly wasn't a genetically-engineered weapon created by a terrorist. Even Professor Duckworth was stunned into silence. A blue cornflower and a white violet had undermined and overturned all his accumulated knowledge of biology.

The answer to the mystery came almost immediately to their surprise from the Ministry of Defence. The appalling muddle between 'Operation Descum' and 'Operation Flying Chestnut' had come to light.

Julianum had come from space.

Excitement ran through the labs like electricity: you could sense it in the air. Everyone felt high with exhilaration.

'It's a fantastic copy!' said John. He held the wild cornflower aloft; a corona of bright blue petals around a black centre on a long stem. He twiddled the stalk in his fingers, spinning the head of the flower.

'But its *not* a copy!' his boss corrected him. 'Think about it . . . it has *become* a cornflower. It *is* a cornflower; not a copy of a cornflower.'

They looked at *Julianum* with new eyes and a new respect.

'Then it must be the best camouflage ever evolved!' said John. 'It copies the DNA of any plant it comes across and imitates the plant exactly . . . sorry . . . I mean *becomes* that plant. And at what a speed! Just think . . . that whole meadow grown in a night. The rate of metabolism is unbelievable!'

'In a sense the word copy *is* right.' Harry Wolf commented thoughtfully. 'You see, that cornflower is a *real* cornflower, but it's made up from very different cells than the sort of cornflowers *we* are used to. Mega–cells with three nuclei. It's a *Julianum* cornflower. *Julianum* must have found seeds of all those meadow flowers deep down in the soil beneath the conventional lawn. They were sleeping there just waiting for the day when man's machinery stopped mowing.'

136

'What rot! You're too romantic, Harry,' Professor Duckworth exploded. 'Waiting for the day indeed! Seeds are seeds not little people!' Then turning to John, 'I'm not so sure about your camouflage theory – looks more like showing off to me! You could hardly miss that meadow!'

His American colleague raised an eyebrow. 'Showing off, Bill? . . . Plants, *showing off*? I thought plants weren't little people!'

Professor Duckworth bellowed a short sharp laugh. 'OK . . . you win. Only a metaphor.'

'And the orchids,' said John. 'They must have been *Julianum* as well. Poor Julia, I wish I'd known at the time. And of course, all those millions of white violets too.'

'It would be interesting to know how they fared in and around Filkins Wood,' added the American. 'Do you think they survived all those horrendous herbicides and fungicides the army hit them with?'

Security was stepped up. The summer vacation at the university had begun so there were few undergraduates about. Those who did stay found themselves being refused access to more than half the campus. The army set up high barricades and the whole area was completely cordoned off. The Ministry of Defence would have liked to have moved the research into *Julianum* to a remoter site but two things militated against such an action. Firstly, the government had closed down its facilities for secret

137

biological and chemical research as part of an international weapons reduction treaty: there was now no obvious place where sensitive research could be carried out. Secondly *Julianum* had already well and truly established itself on the campus. Professor Duckworth was left in charge therefore. The anti-terrorist story, which was supposed to justify the spraying of fungicides, herbicides and agent orange all over a large area of beautiful countryside was allowed to run its course. It would keep the press happy for the time being and so keep the public ignorant of what really had happened in Filkins Wood, though it was only a matter of time before an investigative reporter discovered the truth.

Julia took the phone call from John. He said very little, aware that the phone might be tapped, only asking her to go and see if the white violets were still flowering. She already knew the answer to his question. The white violets beneath the dying hydrangea bush were as fresh as ever. But she decided to go and double check at other spots where they grew.

Julia and Ben had just walked up the lane from where the school bus had dropped them at the road block, when John had rung. Hal walked in five minutes later with Dorothy Garstang.

'Thank God they let those of us who live here drive in and out of the area,' she said. 'No one else is being allowed past the road blocks you

138

know. It would be very awkward if we were imprisoned in our own homes!'

'They take that spraying very seriously – the car had a complete herbicidal car wash . . . even coming *into* the area,' said Hal, 'which seems just a bit illogical!'

'Hal, come with me down the road to the bridge? John wants to know if the white violets survived all that spraying. I said I'd check for him.'

Hal smiled and nodded.

They set off immediately. It was a fifteen minute walk to the bridge and they met two lots of soldiers patrolling the lane. At a road junction they had to submit to boot spraying and to questioning about where they were going. It was all right, they were told, so long as they stayed on the road, kept out of the hedgerows and didn't on any account enter the woods. Locals were permitted to come and go freely, so long as they identified themselves and were prepared to have their footwear sterilised.

Two soldiers kept an eye on them as they walked down the road to where it ran through the narrow strip of woodland with the bridge over the beck.

'No strolling in the woods now!' one of them shouted suggestively.

Julia avoided Hal's eye as she felt herself flush slightly. 'Ignore them,' she muttered.

When they reached the bridge they stopped

and leant over the parapet. Hal pointed downwards but there was no need. Amidst all the dismal decay of dying leaves the carpet of white violets was as astonishing as ever. The leaves of the trees overhanging the stream were all withering, the undergrowth of brambles, bushes and bracken was shrivelled, the mosses decaying; but the vulnerable-looking violets flourished in droves. They gave, even more strongly than before, the appearance of a carpet of snow.

'John said on the phone that they are like the orchids but he didn't explain anything. I think he said they were poly-something. Could that be right? He wouldn't tell me any more. He said it was all top secret and he had to be careful on the phone.'

'I expect he said "polymorphic".'

'That was it,' she looked at him questioningly. Their roles had recently become reversed. Hal was the one with all the explanations; she the one with the questions.

'What he was telling you was that JULIANUM can take on many different shapes. You know . . . it can look like orchids or little yellow flowers (the ones John saw in the lab) or white violets . . .' He trailed off, searching her face to see if she really understood.

'Like a caterpillar can become a butterfly . . . or a tadpole a frog?'

'Sort of . . . you've got the right idea there . . . one set of genes, the DNA, can describe

140

two quite differently shaped creatures. But then *Julianum* is a bit different again . . . I guess it's more adaptable. After all butterflies can't turn back into caterpillars however hard they try.'

'Nor frogs into tadpoles,' she added. 'So *Julianum* can turn into all sorts of flowers . . . isn't that rather unbelievable? I mean it sounds more like magic. I wonder if it can turn into anything else?'

'I met a friend of yours today,' he said, changing the subject. 'In the library in the lunch hour.'

'Who?' she quizzed.

'Bessy? Said she knows you.'

'What was *she* doing in the library at lunchtime?' Julia asked, wishing her voice didn't sound quite so suspicious and cross.

'Changing a book she said. But then she spent the whole time sitting on the table where I was trying to read. She's very insistent isn't she? Every time I turned back to the reference book I was reading she started up a new conversation. I thought people weren't supposed to talk in the library?'

'Sounds *just* like Bessy. I don't know why I ever liked her,' Julia was furious with herself. She had boasted to Betty about Hal, about his interest in everything and his incredible reading abilities. It was typical of Betty to sneak out of school in the lunch hour, without telling her, to go and see him.

'Come on! Let's go and phone John about the white violets!' Julia took Hal by the hand to pull him away from the parapet and to end the annoying conversation about Betty.

A piercing wolf whistle from a soldier up the road made her drop his hand fast. For the second time that evening Julia flushed slightly.

A quarter of an hour later they arrived back at the house.

'Message for you Hal,' called Dorothy Garstang as they entered the back door.

'For me?' he queried.

'Betty . . . says she'll phone back in the next half hour.'

Julia's mouth dropped open.

At that moment the phone rang. Hal answered it; something he had never done before.

Julia made herself busy trying to look uninterested in the telephone conversation. She took a can-opener from the drawer and opened a tin of cat food. As she tipped the contents of the can on to a plate she discovered that Seamus and Finbar had only just been fed five minutes earlier by her mother. Her mother watched her without comment. Hal put the phone down. 'She invited me to go to the cinema with her tonight. Some film called 'Aliens 3'. Hal looked uneasy.

'Do you want to go?' Dorothy Garstang asked.

He was silent for a moment.

'No . . . not really. I'd much rather read all these newspapers I've bought.'

'Then *don't* go,' said Julia.

'But I said I would.'

'And how does Betty expect you to get there?' she asked indignantly, 'the army have stopped the bus running up this way.'

'Oh, she said that if I walked down to the road block at 7.30 her brother would pick me up.'

'She's really got things organised,' muttered Julia.

'You know, you don't have to go,' said Dorothy Garstang, 'and you could have said no.'

'It didn't seem very polite just to say no . . . and anyway she was *very* insistent.'

'I *bet* she was,' said Julia.

'Look – I'll phone,' her mother offered. 'I'll say there was a misunderstanding and that we expected you to be at home tonight.'

'No! *I'll* phone,' Julia said. She sounded so determined that her mother decided not to argue the point. 'After all she's my friend . . . or was my friend.' With that she unplugged the telephone and carried it through to the socket in the hall.

A few minutes later she returned to the kitchen, glowing slightly and with a satisfied smile she tried to disguise.

Without it ever being properly discussed Hal had become part of the family. He fitted into an easy routine and was no trouble to anyone. When Ben and Julia were at school Dorothy Garstang would drop him in town on her way to work so that he could spend the day in the library. Mrs Garstang felt possessive and proud; she had unconsciously adopted him.

Ben had come to admire Hal and to like him: he even found himself feeling pleased when anyone commented on how alike they looked. It was flattering and no longer threatening.

It was Julia who was most affected by Hal's presence in the home and recently her feelings had undergone a transformation. Her father had begun to be concerned about it. After all, he reminded his wife late one night when they were alone, Hal wasn't their son, however much he had become part of the family. Nor had they discovered any more about his origins, who he was or where he had come from. And Julia in his view had become infatuated. His wife's attitude, that a little infatuation never hurt anybody, verged, he felt, on the irresponsible.

It was obvious to Julia more than anyone else that she could not stop thinking about Hal. The hours in school dragged. But then when she got home she felt awkward. It had been easy when Hal needed her to read the newspapers with him, to answer his interminable questions, to watch wild life programmes on the TV with him and to make him feel welcome and at home. Now, although he still seemed to seek out and

144

enjoy her company, he had grown beyond her in many ways.

Instead of going off to do something else when she had nothing to say to Hal, she sat around in the same room just to be with him. Everyone must notice, she supposed, and that made her feel uneasy and self conscious. Life at home began to be claustrophobic for Julia. She wanted to get outside more and more – with Hal of course; but so many of the beautiful walks they could have done were barred by the army and anyway many of the best had been ruined by the spraying. She wished desperately that she could windsurf and sail off on the sea with him like Ben did.

A couple of days after she and Hal had been to check on the white violets Julia had an idea. As soon as she got home from school she would make a picnic supper, get Ben to lend Hal his bike and they would cycle the few miles over to the stables. She had never taken him there before and she was sure he would love to see the horses.

It was a lovely summer afternoon. A light breeze was ideal for cycling: it kept them cool; and blowing in from the sea it was no hindrance as they headed inland. The hills were not steep but some of them were long. The whole evening stretched out ahead of them so they were unhurriedly enjoying the ride. Very soon they were cycling beneath leafy trees and passing copses and hedgerows untouched by the army. In less than an hour they reached the stables.

Hal was as appreciative of the horses as she had expected he would be. He stroked and patted them and was full of admiration. She introduced him to her favourite, Barleymow, and then asked if he would like to ride the horse in the next stable, a fifteen-hands skewbald called Bonnie. Hal was delighted at the idea and after being shown how to mount took the reins, waited for Julia to mount Barleymow, and then set off round the field beside her. He looked immensely confident but he still had to be taught how to canter. He got the idea quickly as he had done with windsurfing, riding with a natural sense of poise and rhythm. For half an hour they cantered around the field together Julia showing him how to approach and then leap over some low jumps.

'I'm hungry! Let's have our picnic,' she suddenly announced.

They hung up the bridles and saddles and then let the horses out into another field. After talking briefly with her friends at the stables they pushed their bikes a little way up the lane to where a large barn was flanked by a bright pond which reflected the sky. They sat on the bank of the pond to eat their picnic and watched farmyard ducks and even a moorhen swim idly across the water. The evening sun was warm.

Cheese and tomato sandwiches, apples, some cake and a bar of chocolate to share. She had thought of making tuna or ham sandwiches, her own favourites, but had noticed recently that, without making an issue out of it, Hal preferred vegetarian food. She reminded herself to point it out to her mother when they got home.

The time came when they should think of cycling back. They had finished the picnic and Julia had suddenly run out of things to say about horses.

'Come on! It's time we went,' she said, scrambling to her feet. She took his hand and pulled him up with such a jerk that he almost fell down the bank into the pond. Laughing, she clung on to him for a second.

'I see! You've had enough of me – you want to drown me while nobody's looking,' he joked.

'Never!' she retorted – rather too seriously she immediately realised and, to hide a sudden flush of self-consciousness, changed the subject quickly. 'Come on! I'll show you a great view, it's in the wrong direction but never mind. It'll only take us five minutes and we don't have to set off home yet.' Home was down-hill most of the way and Julia knew that, once started, they would be there in no time at all.

They pushed their bikes down the track from the barn and out on to the road. Turning right, they mounted and cycled slowly up a steep incline past some woods until they came to the brow of the hill. A great panorama began to open up to their left; a deep river valley, its slopes covered in larch and pine and irregular clumps of broad-leafed trees, cut through the wide curves of fields as they mounted up layer beyond layer to the line of hills on the horizon. Away behind them, just visible as they glanced over their shoulders, the sea glinted in the low evening sunlight. It would soon be sunset.

'Sometimes we ride up this way when we are exercising the horses. It's always beautiful.'

Hal nodded without speaking.

The road swung away to the right, level at first, and then as they came round the bend climbing once more. It was getting late and they ought to be turning back, Julia thought reluctantly, wanting the evening to go on and on. She suddenly stopped and got off her bike. Hal pulled up beside her. 'I think we ought to go back,' she said with a grimace.

'O.K. I suppose so,' Hal agreed with a slight shrug of his shoulders.

They stood looking at each other for several seconds, not wanting to make the decision.

As they turned, before getting back on their bikes, they accidentally swung them in opposite directions and their front wheels collided. It brought them very close for a moment. Afterwards, Julia couldn't remember who had made the first move but, holding on to their bikes with difficulty, each had put an arm round the other and they had kissed.

*

Julia was dejected. She could kill Mrs Lancaster. Why had the woman bothered to phone at all. It was only to say that Blackberry was better; but of course she wouldn't be able to lend him to Julia now that the army had sprayed the countryside? She had decided, in the circumstances, to lend Blackberry to 'that nice girl Antonia' for the rest of the summer. Antonia was far too pleased with herself: she had long hair which she was forever throwing back in the most irritatingly affected manner.

It was one of those long summer evenings when the twilight seems to go on for ever. Julia was kneeling on the chair by the open window, her elbows on the sill and her chin in her hands. The sky was still bright although the fields up behind the house were in shadow. Nevertheless, she could just make out the dark shapes of the jumps she had erected so enthusiastically so many weeks earlier. 'Stop it!' she muttered crossly.

A sound suddenly caught her attention. She cocked her ear to the open window and listened. Had she heard a cuckoo – that broken unfulfilled half-call which the bird sometimes made at the end of its breeding season? She waited, tuning her ears to the remote sounds of a summer's evening: a farm dog barking somewhere, a motorbike in a distant lane; but whatever she had heard was not repeated.

The cuckoo's call was muted with summer.

It no longer uttered its clear notes from the hedgerows that ran down from Filkins Wood: not because of what the army had done to the countryside but in the natural course of things. In April the bird had dominated its breeding territory with a public display of ownership, flying from tree to tree, its voice carrying far in the fresh spring air. But quite soon now, some of the parents would be heading south, migrating back to Africa. A few stragglers and first-year birds might stay on in English woodlands until September; but no later.

April to September: it was a quick season, Julia thought. But it was all the cuckoo needed to breed successfully: taking everything from, but giving nothing in return to, its hosts.

The evening hung heavily. She was fed up. Why, she wondered, did a bad mood always weigh down on her as though it was a sort of 'thing', a burden, like a heavy blanket?

She thought about Hal and yesterday evening. It had all worked out much better than she could have hoped and she had been thrilled to find that he shared her love of horses. But would there be more opportunities to go riding together? If she was honest with herself, she had to admit that it was *that* thought which was depressing her. She had overheard her father saying something to her mother about it being time they all sat down and had a talk. She could guess what they were discussing from the sound of reluctance in her mother's responses. Hal wouldn't be with them for ever.

Hal and Ben were out windsurfing. She had got into an argument with her mother. Her cupboard and her clothes-drawers were in a mess and her mother, as usual, thought it mattered. Julia could never understand why it made her mother so bad tempered. The trouble was, her favourite pair of jeans had mysteriously gone missing. She had searched everywhere – in the laundry basket; amongst the stack of ironing; in her bedroom: they were nowhere to be found. It had taken her hours to stitch three coloured patches to the seat of those jeans: and they were beautifully frayed at the bottoms. Her 'Friends of The Earth' tee shirt had vanished, too. It was when she complained to her mother that she couldn't find them, that the argument had started. Julia had finally retreated to her bedroom.

Gazing out of the window she re-ran once again in her mind, like a tape, her memories of the previous evening: every detail. The uphill bits of the cycle ride and the laughter; Barleymow, Bonnie and conversation at the stables; the picnic and watching the moorhens minding their own business on the bright pond. The kiss. But try as she might she couldn't clearly remember the kiss. She could remember everything leading up to it, to the point where their front wheels had collided. But the kiss itself and what it was actually like eluded her. Every time she reran the tape it became a blur at that precise point. She kicked herself for not being able to remember more clearly.

The sound of a car made her spirits rise and she ran downstairs. The boys had seen a shoal of large jellyfish which they had been careful to avoid. Ben had never seen anything quite like them before.

Hal caught Julia's eye; he seemed to want to say something in private. It was an invitation to go for a walk with him at sunrise.

CHAPTER 13

The Cuckoo Plant

John wondered if perhaps his phone *had* been tapped when he read the banner headline in a national newspaper. 'WHITE VIOLETS IMMUNE TO KILLER SLIME: Top scientists perplexed by the charmed life of the white violet . . .,' ran the article in highly sensational terms. How else could a reporter know so quickly that there was something special about the white violets in Filkins Wood? They had even managed to get a picture of the snow-like carpet of flowers beneath the road bridge over Filkins Beck.

The paper had of course got the story entirely wrong. It was a coordinated attack mounted by a regiment of Her Majesty's armed forces that the white violets had survived. It was still a well-guarded secret that *Julianum* had come from space.

The effect of the news item, however, was to make the tiny flower a very scarce commodity. Posies exchanged hands for £50 or more with a black market running in the cities. The army's overkill of the countryside had made people jittery. Superstitiously, they imagined that the white violet would give some protection from whatever it was that had been let loose by 'the terrorists'. Even some of the soldiers surreptitiously picked small bunches from around Filkins Wood and sent them off to their loved ones or sold them when they were off duty.

Julianum was spreading far and wide. There was no stopping it.

It was dark in the corridor of the zoology department. John knew his way around so the lack of light was no problem. The place was empty. The army would allow no-one, other than those employed on *Julianum*, any access to this part of the university. The only living thing in the building was a snake, a six-foot black mamba which lived in a glass case in Lab.3. The snake had had its poison fangs removed and so it was no danger to anyone. It spent most of its time asleep.

In Lab.3 there was a piece of equipment which John needed rather badly. He opened the door and realised with irritation that the bank of switches for the lights was at the other end of the lab. Somewhere at this end there was a switch for a single light, but all he could remember was that it was in an odd place and not just inside the door.

John stepped into the deeper darkness of the lab and then stopped to get his bearings. He stood for a moment uncertain which way to turn. It was then that he heard a faint sound and realised that something was wrong. He listened.

A soft dry sound of unhurried movement seemed to be coming from the floor in all directions; and from the shelves and cupboards and benches. He didn't recognise it. It was creepy. Quickly he moved to the right searching with his hand for the light switch. Suddenly he caught his foot in something on the floor and tripped. As luck would have it he fell against the wall and almost instantly found the switch he was looking for.

Light flooded the room. John gasped and froze to the spot. The whole lab was a seething mass of black mambas slithering and sliding across each other, coiling and uncoiling themselves around the equipment and the furniture. The floor was a snake pit.

He noticed with horror that one of the longest snakes, hanging from some shelves only two feet from his head was eyeing him with interest. This was not the tired old black mamba which slept out its days in the case above the radiator. The snake moved slowly, glossy scaled, alert and alive. It curved its neck and drew up its head to stare straight into John's face. For a moment he felt too terrified to move or even to breathe.

John hesitated for a second and then leapt for

the exit. A shiver of shock ran up his spine as he slammed the door shut behind him. He was fortunate to have escaped; several snakes had been curling around his feet.

Julianum was coming up with new surprises; it didn't just turn itself into harmless flowers he reflected.

'We've no idea whether it's friendly or hostile,' pondered Professor Duckworth. He looked out of the lab window at the deepening twilight.

'Or just plain neutral,' drawled his American colleague. 'Why should it be any more hostile than a geranium for heaven's sake? Maybe it just grows and does its own thing? So it turned itself into a load of snakes but they didn't hurt anyone.'

'Not yet!' answered John. 'Those snakes were complete with poison fangs!'

'And locusts do their own thing,' said Professor Duckworth. 'A plague of them settled in Morocco last month. Those poor farmers could be forgiven for thinking of them as hostile!'

'True,' his friend conceded.

A new dimension had been added to their research by the discovery that *Julianum* could take the form of a black mamba. It was a fact they found hard to believe. A lady's slipper orchid, a white violet, a blue cornflower were all intricate enough, but the internal structure of a snake was of a different order. Its nervous system for a start,

156

which controlled the ripple flow of its muscles, alerted it to danger or braced it for a kill, was much more complicated than anything found in the passive life of a plant.

The episode of the snakes reinforced the Ministry of Defence's view that *Julianum* posed a great threat to the life of the nation which should be taken very seriously. A plant which could transform itself into an epidemic of deadly poisonous snakes could be the plague to end all plagues. No time was to be wasted.

The task now facing Professor Duckworth and his team of researchers was to find, as quickly as possible, something that could be guaranteed to kill *Julianum*.

Conventional herbicides, fungicides, pesticides or poisons were useless. If anything, *Julianum* seemed to thrive on them. 'Showing off again!' was Professor Duckworth's regular comment as the slime devoured yet another poisonous chemical in a test tube.

The answer had to be a virus.

The only known virus, which almost certainly would do the job of killing *Julianum*, existed in very small quantities. It was stored in a secret location known only to a handful of people. It was Omega-zed, the lethal product of some genetic engineering for biological warfare conducted by a government establishment some years earlier. As far as was known, Omega-zed could invade the system of any organism, plant or animal, and so disrupt it as to cause certain and rapid death. Trials had been 100% successful.

When international weapons treaties had finally called a halt to all biological warfare research, small quantities of Omega-zed had been hoarded in secret – just in case the need for it arose. The dubious moral argument being that other countries were probably doing the very same thing.

No one had any idea how it would fare if released into the environment. It was impossible to predict the damage it might do. The worst scenario its creators could imagine was that it could wipe out all life on Earth. Military strategists had argued; either it was useless because no one would be mad enough to use it (that would be suicide), or else it was the ultimate deterrent and could be used to hold any potential aggressor up to ransom.

The Doomsday virus, as it had been nicknamed, was to be resurrected, reproduced and stockpiled in a remote house on a Scottish island owned by the Ministry of Defence: just in case *Julianum* posed a real threat to the world. Omega-zed would be a last resort. Professor Duckworth and his team would make absolutely certain first of all that no other virus could do the job. Earth was potentially a hostile environment for a creature from space. Just as traders and missionaries had been known to devastate the populations of remote tribes by unwittingly introducing diseases from Europe to which they had built up no resistance, so there might be naturally occurring viruses which would decimate *Julianum*. A variety of the common cold virus, or of flu, or perhaps of tobacco leaf mould might be all that was needed to kill the protoplasm.

'You realize the consequences of this?' The professor asked his colleagues. 'If *Julianum* can imitate a snake . . . and not just imitate but *become* a snake . . . then it can become other creatures too perhaps. Just like it became a meadow of wild flowers.'

Harry Wolf was holding up a test tube of harmless-looking protoplasm which had just consumed a concentrated dose of arsenic.

'You know,' he pondered aloud, 'there could be a whole *zoo* in here, a whole Noah's ark of creatures and maybe some we've never seen before. Suppose it's trick is this,' he speculated. 'Whenever it comes across a new life form it collects a copy of its DNA. Rather like a book collector collecting books. Then it stores the DNA in one of its own nuclei depending on whether it's an animal, a plant, or something else?'

'Like an actor collecting disguises? It's a neat theory,' pondered Professor Duckworth. 'Life on another world could have come up with all sorts of tricks.'

'So what is *Julianum* – animal, plant or

fungus?' the American asked shaking his head. 'We're going to have a big classification problem here!'

'That's the least of our worries. If we don't find a way to control it soon then some fool in the army is going to use Omega–Zed! And that will be life on earth's *last* trick! What an irony!' he went on. 'It may be a harmless plant. A sort of 'Cuckoo Plant' if you like, borrowing our DNA like a cuckoo borrows other birds' nests. It may be a wonderful addition to our native flora and fauna. And then we go and wipe ourselves out with a lethal virus trying to kill it!'

Harry Wolf nodded slowly in agreement.

'It was well named . . . The Doomsday Virus!'

An urgent expression suddenly crossed John's face.

'Heh! We've been so *blind*! He must be laughing at us right now!'

The two professors looked at him for an explanation.

'*We* are animals!'

'So?' the American queried.

'So . . . if *Julianum* can imitate a blue cornflower and now a black mamba, then what's to stop it imitating a person? If your theory is right then it would only have to get hold of some human DNA from a mouth swab or from a pricked finger and *Julianum* could *become* a person.' The memory of Ben being pricked in the palm of his hand by the weird fish in Filkins Pool flashed across his mind.

There was silence as they pondered the possibility. It was hard to imagine that, outside the pages of science fiction, such a thing could really happen. Cloning people, making exact copies of them from extracted DNA, was a fantasy from the distant future.

'Nothing,' said his boss. 'There's nothing to stop it . . . except . . .,' he thought a bit more, '. . . except nothing. In principle it *could*. What do you think, Harry?'

'It's a staggering thought. Up to this moment I would have dismissed the idea out of hand. So would you, Bill. But we're dealing with an extraordinary organism. But if *Julianum* can copy people like it can copy flowers or snakes there would have to be a difference.'

'What do you mean?'

'Well think about it. A cornflower doesn't have to *learn* how to be a cornflower. And a snake's behaviour is programmed in its DNA. But there's much more to a person. A person has to grow in a culture; a person has to be introduced to conversation and ideas; a person has to learn language and all the subtleties of human behaviour. That's why children need such long secure childhoods – there's so much to learn about *how* to be human. There's an awful lot that's not stored in the DNA.'

Professor Duckworth nodded.

'It would have to *be* a cuckoo – find a foster family and learn its culture there. And a lot would depend on how fast it could learn.'

'Exactly,' said John looking anxious. 'I was thinking of Hal.'

His family was being used by *Julianum*. But for what? They could not guess. One thing was certain, however, Hal was the key.

CHAPTER 14

Morning Glories

It was a bright morning and very early. The rising sun flooded across the landscape and into the bedroom window. Julia woke in a strange mood. She had dreamed that something had woken her and she had gone to the window and looked up over the fields to Filkins Wood. An old half moon had risen beyond the tree line.

There was movement around the edge of the woods and although far away and in shadow, she knew what she was seeing. A wave of horsemen had ridden out from under the trees. They galloped down across the fields into the faint moonlight flying over gateway and hedgerow. Julia opened the window and let in the fresh night air. She could hear the thunder of hooves as the horsemen swept through the fields, past the house and on down to the sea.

That wave had been followed by another and then another . . .

The dream had seemed very real: one of those

163

dreams which leaves its mood with you well into the day, and the images are more pressing than things seen when awake.

Julia leant out of her bedroom window and wondered about her dream. She scanned the dark stricken outline of Filkins Wood for any sign of movement. All was still. She thought of the mysterious pool deep amongst the trees, its water quietly trickling over into Filkins Beck. The early morning sky was empty of clouds: only a pale half-moon was to be seen, white and ghost like in the broad expanse of blue.

She dressed quickly. No one else was about. A piece of paper on the floor by the bedroom door caught Julia's eye. It was a note written in a straight bold hand. 'Come up to Filkins Wood. It's safe now. I've gone on ahead. Go up by the muddy lane and keep close to the edge of the fields. The soldiers won't see you if you go that way. They have got lazy! See you at the pool. What a beautiful morning! Love. Hal.'

After only a moment's hesitation Julia crept out of the house closing the back door quietly behind her.

The woods were silent; skeleton trees had shed their poisoned leaves. Brittle twigs snapped underfoot; moss and lichen on the rocks had withered; the bracken was dead.

Such a stupid mess, she thought to herself, as she surveyed the ugly effects of the poisonous chemicals everywhere. It made no sense. If

Julianum had been washed down to the sea then there seemed no point in killing everything else. The army had made a mistake which they weren't admitting: she knew that. But if the protoplasm just turned itself into beautiful flowers then why was everyone still treating it as top secret? How could anyone find orchids and white violets threatening? She felt very confused and rather uneasy. After all, it was she who had provided the sample of *Julianum* which had led to all the fuss. It had even been named after her. The army had made war on *her* plant.

'Morons!' she muttered as she set off deeper into the woods. 'Ignorant . . . stupid . . . morons!'

And why wasn't Hal anywhere to be seen? He might at least have waited for her at the edge of the wood, she thought crossly. And why had he left the house before her anyway, and gone on ahead, considering that it was he who had invited her to join him on an early morning walk? She wanted to call his name but caution kept her quiet. No-one had seen her come this far: it would be a pity to spoil things now, by shouting and attracting the attention of the soldiers who were supposed to be on duty.

Then she stopped as she suddenly caught the strong smell of violets. Off to her right a broad carpet of white violets spread out between the trees; beautiful – but even more astonishing, and causing her to catch her breath, was the violet haze that stretched away beyond them. Millions of the more common variety of violet covered the woodland floor. It was they she supposed that were source of the scent.

Strange if they, too, were all *Julianum*: *her* flowers . . .

Julia walked on and noticed to her surprise that the further she penetrated the woodland the more green vegetation she came across; leaves and fronds that looked familiar and others she had never seen before. Ferns sprouted from the roots of trees while strange broad leafed plants erupted exotically on every side; great fountains of fresh greenery replacing and overrunning the dead undergrowth. Other plants spread creeper like over rocks and old tree stumps. Soon she was wading thigh deep through tall grasses and wild herbage. A profusion of leaves of every shape surrounded her on every side.

Julia stood still, astonished. Was all this *Julianum* too?

A gentle rustling behind her caught her attention and made her turn round.

Flowers were blooming back along the way she had just come. Buds she had not noticed were quietly popping and unfurling in every direction. It was as though by walking through all this fresh vegetation Julia had somehow triggered a wave of blossom.

She recognised orchids, wood anemones and patches of willow herb. Amongst them were other flowers which were unfamiliar; constellations of tiny white stars clustered together in patches; discreet blue trumpets on delicate slender stalks hid in the shadows; deep red blooms heavy headed like peonies drooped close to the ground. It was a gorgeous sight. Even in the subdued light of the woodland it was a richer and more colourful display than in many an herbaceous border in any garden known to her.

New blooms unfurled their petals as she watched. They *must* be *Julianum*, all of them, Julia concluded.

A yellow butterfly fluttered into a shaft of sunlight and landed on a purple bough of buddleia.

The transformation of the undergrowth had been so sudden that she wondered if she was still in bed dreaming. The woodland of leafless trees had become a paradise glowing with colour. Perhaps this was another part of the strange dream in which waves of horsemen had ridden out from the woods and down to the sea. It had the same atmosphere; she was filled with the same feeling of contentment, an observer watching something happen which was good. She pinched herself to see; but then felt silly. If it was a dream then it would be a dream pinch and that would tell her nothing. Yet, strange as it all was, it seemed very much *unlike* a dream. These were definitely real flowers she thought, as she bent down to smell an unusual bloom with a fragrance as sweet as a wallflower.

The thought of the pool beckoned her. She began to pick her way carefully between the tree trunks, the patches of flowers and the rocks, most of which were festooned with climbing and trailing vegetation. The woodland ought to be growing even lighter ahead where the rugged hillside began to rise up towards the outcrops of stone where Filkins Pool lay calm and still. Instead it grew darker.

Julia peered cautiously into the darkness. It was unexpected. Then she saw why.

Everything was overhung with creepers, whole thickets and curtains of twining stems hanging down beneath the trees; more canopies of creeper draping from branch to branch darkening the sky. All this was new. She struggled forward slowly, ducking now and then to avoid the drooping skeins of woody rope.

A movement caught her eye. A black cat ran through the jungle of undergrowth. It ignored her and ran up and over a steep bit of bank disappearing quickly from view. A second cat followed almost immediately: Seamus and Finbar. She called after them; and waited; but they were gone.

There was a light up ahead in the direction of the pool; a patch of sunshine breaking through the branches she guessed. Her hair got caught at that moment in a creeper and she had to spend a minute or two unhooking it. It had got snagged in what appeared to be a tight cluster of sticky buds. Once free, Julia pulled herself up the final difficult climb to the pool.

It was the tree that struck her first of all. It was growing at the top of the vertical rock face which plunged down into the water at the far side of the pool. Its broad leaves were the pale yellow of cowslips; but the extraordinary thing about them was that they shone with their own light.

A breeze stirred the leaves of the tree and ripples of light ran up and down the trunk. The same zephyr brushed the surface of the pool and the tree's reflection shimmered for a moment and then settled again.

'The sunbeam tree!' said a voice close by.

Julia jumped with a startled 'Oh!'

Hal was standing a little off to her left. He was by the edge of the pool leaning idly against the white trunk of a slender silver birch. Two black cats sat on mounds of green moss one on each side of him. Julia had never seen Hal looking so like her brother Ben before.

The gust of breeze which had stirred the sunbeam tree was followed by a faint restless murmuring. It came from all sides. Julia, pricking up her ears, was about to ask Hal if he could hear it too when turning her head this way and that she let out a gasp of astonishment.

The creepers were coming to life everywhere; leaves unfurling, buds visibly swelling and bursting. They formed a dense curtain so that the area around the pool, the rocks and a few free standing trunks, was enclosed as though in a secret garden. As the blooms opened, a wave of blue, starting at ground level, ran up through the trees: the blue of morning glories and of the sky.

The sunbeam tree bathed the whole transformed scene in soft light.

'What?' she began, amazed and bewildered. She was confused, but somehow knew that Hal would be able to answer her unasked questions. She sat down on a moss covered rock at the very edge of the pool.

'What is all this – and why isn't it dead from the poison?' was all she could manage.

'It's all *Julianum*,' he answered with a smile. 'And it's not dead because the poisons acted like fertilisers! Funny isn't it? – all those chemical killers that the army sprayed!'

Julia gazed at him in silence.

'Do you like it?' he asked. 'It's all my garden!'

'*Your* garden? . . . But how can it be?' Suddenly all sorts of questions were crowding together in her head and Julia was bursting to ask them. 'Was all that stuff we found in the pool yours too? . . . and all the white violets?' and then she added quickly, 'And why do you look so like Ben?'

She wished that the last question had not sounded quite so like an accusation. Embarrassed, she looked down into the water but all she could see was her own reflection and the inverted image of the glowing sunbeam tree.

170

'A *bit* like him – but not entirely like him,' Hal replied by way of an answer.

'How did you plant all this?' Julia continued. 'And when? The army have kept people away . . . and I never knew you came up here anyway.'

'Not *plant* exactly,' he answered slowly, '. . . although I *am* the gardener. But then you see I am also the garden.'

Julia looked puzzled.

'*You* are the garden? What do you mean?'

'The plants, the flowers . . . and everything else; and me. We're all one. We are all *Julianum*.'

'All those white violets . . .' she began.

Hal nodded.

'I *am* the white violets,' he said simply.

Julia lapsed into silence. She let his words sink in: they were crazy and yet she believed him. They made sense: and yet they made no sense at all. Her eyes returned to the pool. It, too, was impenetrable. Bright reflections of the sky and the sunbeam tree made it difficult to see anything beneath the surface.

'Here – let me show you something,' said Hal; and with that he climbed over some boulders and scrambled up the steep bank that flanked the overhanging rock face at the far side of the pool. He disappeared for a moment behind the shoulder of rock and then re-emerged by the trunk of the sunbeam tree.

'Look – it has fruit,' he called down. Hal

held back a branch so that she could see as he picked.

'Catch!' he called as he lobbed a piece of fruit down to her.

Julia leant forward to catch it but she missed and it landed in the pool with a splash, spraying her with a sparkle of water.

'Oh!' she squeaked and then stretched out to salvage the creamy-coloured fruit as it bobbed to the surface beside her. Water ran off its waxy skin in large drops. It smelt strange but appetising.

'Peel it . . . it's quite safe,' Hal called. 'You'll like it.'

The peel came away easily like the shell of an autumn chestnut. The grey-blue fruit from inside smelt even more delicious. At first she nibbled experimentally and found it firm but yielding; then she boldly sank her teeth into the succulent flesh. An explosion of sweetness filled her mouth.

'Mmm . . . fantastic!' she murmured with her mouth full. 'It's like nothing on earth!'

'Quite right! It's new to earth!'

Hal stood by the sunbeam tree gazing down at her. He looked pleased with her enjoyment.

Julia took another bite and let herself be lost in the flood of flavour.

'Welcome to the garden!' he called down. 'By eating *Julianum* you become part of *Julianum* and *Julianum* becomes part of you.'

172

Julia was too taken with the taste of the fruit to give any thought to what Hal had just said. It was all so exquisitely extraordinary that she preferred not to think too hard for a while.

A delicate scent wafted down from the curtains of blue flowers that were draped from the trees all around. Julia became aware of it as it mingled with the extraordinary taste of the fruit of the sunbeam tree.

A piece of peel she had dropped into the pool began to bob up and down. She watched intently until she saw that it was being nibbled by a silver fish. Then with a flurry of water another smaller fish leapt up out of the pool; but instead of falling back into the water it hung suspended in the air like a humming bird. A second silvery minnow followed and then another. Within half a minute a whole shoal of tiny fish were flicking and gliding gracefully through the air around her. Effortlessly weaving their way to and fro amongst the trees, they finally disappeared through the curtains of creeper as though into forests of blue seaweed.

Julia was speechless.

The dry clean stone of the fruit she had eaten still lay in her hand. She had been clutching it for ages. She threw it a few feet from her into the dark water and watched to see if she could follow it as it sank through the reflections.

'I did think of not telling you any of this.'

Hal looked almost apologetic as he sat down

on the moss covered rock beside her. Seamus and Finbar brushed against their legs purring and demanding attention. Julia picked up Finbar and hugged him.

'I've been so happy living in your home and you've taught me so much . . . you've taught me to be human – you and Ben and your mum and dad . . . and Mrs B.! But I've got to go. A bit of me wants to stay – very much. But I can't.'

Julia frowned. 'Why? I don't understand.'

'Plenty of people will tell you – and quite soon. And that's why I have to go. In a way I'd like to pretend that I'm just a visitor who was fortunate enough to stay in your home – and then we could be friends for always. But now other people know about me – they've guessed – and so everything is changed.' He paused and looked straight at her. 'It's the first time I've felt really unhappy; I've felt lonely before – and sometimes a bit frightened; but never unhappy.'

Hal put his arms round her and gave her a long hug. Then he told her she should go straight home. She'd been in the woods longer than she imagined – they would be wondering at home where she was.

'Will we see you again?' asked Julia.

Hal smiled. 'I promise.'

CHAPTER 15

A Scarlet Flush

Julia was surprised to find that a thin mist was rising from the ground as she left the woods. It was unseasonal; an unexpected hint of autumn lying in wraiths along the leafless hedgerows, obscuring distant detail and dampening the ground with dew. She walked down across the middle of the field not caring any longer who saw her. An armful of flowers, a great bouquet of *Julianum*, was for her mother.

How would she explain to them all the things that Hal had told her? Coming from him, in the extraordinary garden that had grown up around Filkins Pool, it had made a sort of sense – even if it also seemed unbelievable. And here were the flowers to prove it.

The need to take a bath was the ideal excuse for not going into lengthy explanations when she arrived home; at least for the moment.

The mist was gathering into dense patches and

thickening into fog when John arrived unannounced at the Garstangs' back door, half an hour later. Julia was still upstairs. John's dilemma, as they had driven north in the fast car provided by the military, was whether or not to phone ahead and warn his family about Hal. Professor Duckworth had decided that they should keep these suspicions entirely to themselves, for the time being. After the ghastly episode of the spraying of agent orange he felt it would be wiser not to share with anyone their ideas about the possibility of *Julianum* transforming itself into people.

Whether Hal would be at home when they arrived had been a matter of some speculation. Harry Wolf had taken out a large bet with his friends. 'Bill, he'll be way ahead of us,' he had argued. 'If his IQ is anything to go by, he'll have worked out by now that we know – and he'll have guessed that we know that he knows that we know! He'll just be waiting for us to catch up!'

Julianum seemed to be able to transform itself into flowers without any external assistance – and even into snakes. But a person? They agreed that some sort of master mind or complex genetic programme would be needed to guide the growth of an intelligent human being.

Everything pointed to the pool. The whole strange episode stemmed from there. Naval divers had therefore been sent to investigate.

But how much should they be told? Should they be made aware of the possibility that some sort of intelligence was lurking deep in the 'bottomless' pool? Professor Duckworth had finally decided that the men should at least be warned that the mission could be very dangerous. But he discovered that they had already anticipated the potential hazards of the mission.

Dorothy Garstang opened the door wide to let them in and fog curled visibly over their shoulders as they quickly entered. She shut the door immediately.

'John! What a surprise! Why didn't you let us know you were coming? Did you bring this horrible fog with you?' she asked, giving her son a kiss.

'It was clear and dry all the way north until we turned off the main road about three miles back,' he replied.

'Then we hit it!' said Professor Duckworth.

'What a welcome eh?' added Harry Wolf with a grin.

'It was across the road like a wall,' said John. 'We came round a corner and there it was! There was no mention of it on the weather forecast on the radio. And you know it's so thick we kept driving off the road!'

Then taking his mother by the arm he lowered his voice. 'Where's Hal? We need to speak to him. It's urgent.'

'Oh dear, you've just missed him,' she said

with a frown. 'Julia saw him last – early this morning and he told her he was leaving.'

'I guessed!' Harry interrupted.

'What's the matter . . . he's not in trouble is he?'

'No . . . not exactly. It's more complicated than that. It'll take a bit of explaining.'

Outside the fog got worse as the morning wore on. A soldier could barely see his own hand held at arm's length. Men on duty at checkpoints could see nothing of the centre of the road they were guarding. Other soldiers sent to relieve them inched their way cautiously through the murky gloom. Torchlight was useless: the fog splayed the beam straight back at the person holding the torch. The air was damp and smelt of fungus and wet earth.

The team of naval commandos in three land-rovers, with a truck full of diving equipment, generators and arc lights, following behind, were stuck in the fog.

At one o'clock Ben turned on the TV news to see why the weather was behaving so strangely. It was mentioned only briefly as an unusual patch of dense fog by the coast. Traffic was advised to avoid the area. People at the Weather Bureau were puzzled.

The item was completely overshadowed, however, by a much more dramatic story concerning an American aircraft carrier far out on the

Atlantic. Everyone, including the two professors, clustered round the TV set.

The U.S.S. *John F. Kennedy* was one of the most powerful battle stations afloat and one of the largest aircraft carriers in the American Navy: a prodigious war machine. It was virtually unsinkable. Guided missile cruisers and destroyers bristling with guns escorted the U.S.S. *John F. Kennedy* wherever she went. Some of the destroyers' guns packed such a punch that they could hurl shells, weighing half a ton a-piece, well over the visible horizon. Nothing, short of a direct hit from a nuclear bomb, could halt the U.S.S. *John F. Kennedy* from cutting its chosen path through the oceans of the world: or so it was firmly believed.

The ship boasted ninety-five planes. Banks of jet fighters were parked neatly on deck while others were stored away ready to be shunted up into the open by hydraulic lifts and catapulted into the sky at a moment's notice. Helicopters were poised to take off at any time to buzz around the ship like angry wasps.

Five thousand crew members, from admiral down to cleaner, lived and worked on the great ship in an ant's nest of ordered activity. It was their floating city; a mechanical moveable city which could quickly position itself in any of the oceans of the world where American interests were thought to be threatened. America was proud of her.

Everyone assumed, until early that summer morning, that the great battle station was invincible. But then they hadn't reckoned on *Julianum*.

A gigantic raft of water lilies had appeared in the night. The great aircraft carrier and the whole fleet of minesweepers and destroyers had been immobilised in the early hours of the day. They were trapped.

Spectacular film taken from a reconnaissance plane showed that a hundred square miles of Atlantic was green and scarlet with leaves and flowers. It was estimated that there could be upwards of a hundred billion tons of vegetation floating round the marooned aircraft carrier and its escort vessels. Satellite pictures revealed that the fresh blush on the face of the Atlantic could be seen even from space.

An eyewitness on board the carrier described how the Atlantic had been transformed into a vast green heaving lily pond in a matter of minutes. The leaves and flowers seemed to have been lurking in the depths until all at once they pushed their way dripping out of the water. The admiral had ordered depth charges to be dropped to clear a path. It had been useless.

'*Julianum*,' said Harry Wolf in a loud voice from the doorway where he was standing watching the TV. 'And a 100 billion tons of it!'

'Bit ironic isn't it!' chuckled Professor Duckworth. '. . . The army sprays the countryside with agent orange to kill the stuff – and then it goes and arrests the largest and most expensive war machine afloat!'

'Very specific targeting I should say Bill! Boy! I bet that admiral's mad!'

'Question is . . . is it an act of aggression or of self-defence? Are the water lilies hostile or just protecting their own? And this weird fog . . . I bet *Julianum*'s got something to do with this too.' He looked at the window where nothing could be seen beyond the glass but light-less murk.

'I'm sure *Julianum* doesn't want to *hurt* any-body,' said Julia. She had told them all she knew about Hal, what he had said to her that morning and all she had seen. She had even recounted her dream of the waves of horsemen riding down to the sea. Suddenly her dream seemed rather prophetic.

The American looked at her thoughtfully for a moment. He was no longer sure of his pet theory that aliens from space would be friendly and not hostile. They might just be uncaring and amoral.

'So O.K. – he was a nice guy. I believe you. But nice guys aren't always good guys. And you say he's clever; but genius isn't a guarantee of generosity. Look . . . we're dealing here with a life form we've never come across before. We know nothing about its behaviour or its ethics – if it has any. For all we know it could be playing

181

cat and mouse with us . . . just playing around until its got itself well-established . . . and got *us* well staked out.'

'So *this* is the way the world will end,' said Professor Duckworth, 'not with a bang but a rustle of leaves!'

'You see, Julia,' said John 'it's not that we think *Julianum* will deliberately harm us, but life has developed on earth by the survival of the fittest. Darwin called it Natural Selection. This extraordinary stuff may be much more advanced than we are. It may quietly take over the entire planet. Without intending to, it might drive mankind to extinction . . . like people caused the dodo to die out.'

'They *hunted* the dodo . . . easy meat for the settlers in Madagascar,' corrected Professor Duckworth.

'O.K., Bill,' John agreed. 'But there are hundreds of other species, as we all know, which have died out specifically because of what human beings have done . . . ploughing up their habitats, polluting their waters, pillaging their forests.'

The professor nodded. 'You're right of course.'

'The point is,' John continued, 'we didn't intend to wipe all those creatures out – it just happened. *Julianum* might do the same to us without meaning to.'

'I still think it wouldn't,' Julia replied with stubborn conviction. 'And *Julianum* isn't just "it"; it's "*he*". Hal cares about things – about people and plants – about *everything* – ask anybody.'

'What was it he said?' asked the American. 'I am the white violets. I am the gardener. I am the garden?' He paused for a moment. Then his face suddenly lit up.

'Bill! I just realised what he's saying! *Julianum* isn't just a plant which can take on many shapes . . . we've got the wrong idea completely. It's a total ecosystem! It's not a single species, it's a whole *set* of species and sub-species. A sort of complete Garden of Eden.'

'Garden of Eden?'

Harry Wolf nodded furiously. 'Flowers, insects, trees, animals, people – the lot! A sort of travelling park. That fireball was a giant seed, a sort of . . . what shall we call it? . . . an ecopod. What a brilliant way to travel through the galaxy! No need for a complicated spaceship. No need for trained astronauts, or provisions or equipment – just one pod, one seed! That must be *the* ultimate in genetic engineering! Fantastic!'

'An ecopod . . . a Garden of Eden seed,' Professor Duckworth repeated thoughtfully. 'That's quite an idea Harry. But if *Julianum* is the Garden of Eden then let's hope we don't turn out to be the weeds!' He paused. 'Maybe we can co-exist . . . both live on the planet . . . like cat and dogs live in the same house together with people. There could be room for both of us. It would certainly change world politics! But if we can't co-exist then Omega-Zed may be the answer after all.'

'Omega-Zed?' queried Julia.

Next morning the fog lifted with the sunrise. First the tree trunks appeared and then their branches; the fog became a low cloud breaking up in the early morning breeze and dispersing. The sun shining through the last faint wisps of mist caught the dripping hedgerows and made them glisten.

The commandos had spent a cramped night in their landrovers. They woke and moved fast. The mysterious nature of their mission was exhilarating. After consulting a large scale Ordinance Survey map they set off up a lane and then across fields. In a very short time they had reached the perimeter of Filkins Wood. They parked their vehicles by the fence in the shadow of the great beech trees. The truck with the generator trundled up slowly behind them.

It was decided to make a reconnaissance before rolling out the cable for the underwater lights. They set off at a jog into the woods, first over the bare woodland floor where all plants and undergrowth had been killed and then through luxurious banks of new vegetation. Exotic blooms were thrust aside as they made their way to where they judged the pool to be. Eventually one of the party located it having found Filkins Beck and followed its course upstream. He called to the others.

They gazed in astonishment at the sunbeam tree as they stood in a half circle around the edge of the pool and listened to a strange sound. It was strange because it was unexpected: the echoing splash of a distant stream deep in a dark cave.

Filkins Pool was empty: a great gaping hole in the floor of the woods, a cavern so deep that they could not see the bottom as they peered cautiously over the edge and down into the darkness.

The men all had potholing experience and within half an hour they had rigged up lights and ropes. They abseiled over the wet rocks past the last of the tree roots and down into hillside. They had dropped into another world, a spacious subterranean realm of dark wet rock and uneven surfaces alternately shining and then falling into shadow as the lights swung on the cables. The cave broadened out beneath the hill into a vast cavern and the men's voices echoed as they called to each other.

The rocks were split and faulted. Deep fissures ran into the hill, dark and narrow – too narrow for a man to explore. From one of these fissures there bubbled a spring of water. It tumbled down over the jumble of rocks below. Here was the source of Filkins Beck. It would take weeks if not months to fill the cave again. Even now the men could not see the floor of the cavern: great slabs of rock lay across deeper crevices and dripping corridors of darkness. High above them they could see their ropes and cables snaking away to a small circular path of light – the sky.

Whatever had been in Filkins Pool had gone, under the cover of fog, and taken all the water with it.

It was only later as the men emerged from the woods that they had time to notice a great swathe of white violets running down across the open field and on into the next field and beyond: a broad carpet of flowers, a royal road running right down to the sea.

CHAPTER 16

Black Tulips

'They – make – me – so – *angry*!' exploded Ben.

Julia was mortified.

Spread out in front of them on the kitchen table were three national newspapers. A large photo of a tearful Julia trying to hide her face from the camera dominated the front page of one of them. In the picture, she was standing at their back door with her father, who had one arm around her. He wore a worried expression.

DISTRESSED FAMILY DECEIVED BY ALIEN – was the caption.

'It wasn't Hal that distressed me,' said Julia furiously. 'It was those awful reporters with their stupid mean questions – "Are you bitter?" "What was it like to sit at table with a boy made of protoplasm?" "Did he make any advances to you?" – and you know what they were getting at! – I hate them all.' She had difficulty in suppressing more tears.

'Don't worry,' said Ben, 'some papers will print anything just to catch the eye. There'll be new editions tomorrow and these ones will be in the dustbin.'

'Well, I'm putting this one in the dustbin *now*,' she said and rolled the newspaper up in fury.

'Here – look!' said Ben when his sister returned from disposing of the offending newspaper. He hoped to divert her attention from the more painful columns. In front of him a double-page spread in colour showed the American aircraft carrier marooned in its raft of water lilies. The ocean was scarlet with flowers.

'What a fantastic sight! They're beautiful,' said Julia smiling at last.

'I bet that's not what the U.S. navy thinks!'

The immobilising of the U.S.S. *John F. Kennedy* had been a watershed. From then on it had been impossible for the Ministry of Defence to keep the media happy with false cover stories. The news was out. Earth had been visited by a mysterious alien life form from outer space.

FLOWER POWER ran the headline in one tabloid: others were more sinister; MONSTER PLANT INVADES EARTH; THE END OF MANKIND?; GREENHOUSE KILLERS – EXOTIC PLANT FROM SPACE. The article which Julia enjoyed most and which she read aloud to Ben began 'CUCKOO PLANT: Mysterious metamorphosis of a seed from the Garden of Eden'. The reporter had based her column on an interview with Harry Wolf; it was accurate, cautious and well-written, carrying no hint of scaremongering or speculation about evil aliens.

For days, camera teams, reporters and photographers swarmed everywhere: they waylaid politicians in Whitehall; they hired planes to fly over the floating island of water lilies in the Atlantic; they invaded the countryside and villages around Filkins Wood (the army prevented them from actually entering the woods themselves); they camped out around the perimeter of John's university where the armed guard had to be doubled. Two policemen were even needed on permanent duty at the Garstangs' gate to protect them from voracious reporters hungry for a new slant on the story.

Only Omega-Zed remained top secret. Julia and Ben were not surprised to find no reference to it. Military secrets were protected by the law.

The Garstang family were under siege. Ben and Julia could not go to school – 'until the fuss has blown over' as a local police chief had said with remarkable understatement. Meanwhile their parents had to run the gauntlet of a barrage of photographers, who had staked out the house, every time they set off for work or went into town. Mrs B., who loved the drama and liked to be at the centre of things, spent far more time with them than usual; she had appointed herself official answerer of the telephone and took great delight in fending off journalists – unless she was the one they wanted to talk to.

While the siege of journalists continued for the Garstangs, the siege of flowers ended for the American aircraft carrier. After three days of frustration, the U.S.S. *John F. Kennedy* with her convoy of escort ships suddenly found themselves free. The gigantic raft of water lilies released its hostages. They disappeared as mysteriously as they had come, quietly closing their blooms in the night and submerging beneath the waves. Next morning the Atlantic was grey and rough and open. The admiral ordered the nuclear engines to be started. Cautiously the great ship moved forward and picked up speed. A sigh of relief spread through the upper decks and someone quipped that with any luck it would be mermaids next time.

Several days later, when the press seemed at last to have grasped the point that neither would the Garstangs be giving any more interviews nor would they sell their story exclusively to one newspaper, the phone rang. Only Ben and Julia were are home although two policemen on duty sat in a car at the gate to guarantee their privacy. Julia felt uneasy about answering it but Ben, lying in the sun at the top of the garden, was obviously making no move.

She continued to hesitate but the phone was insistent. It might be Hal. She was longing to hear from him. The possibility overcame her doubts and she picked up the handset.

'Julia!' said a friendly male voice.

'Yes?' she answered hopefully.

'You don't know me – but I wondered if I could help in any way . . .'

Julia's heart sank. Another reporter she thought to herself wearily and was about to put down the receiver with the usual brisk formula 'no comment', when she heard the speaker saying something about her headmistress Mrs Kendall.

'. . . and you know, she's having sleepless nights over you?'

It seemed so unlikely she had to hear more.

'. . . She can't get over how *mean* the press have been to you over this affair – and especially to *you* Julia.'

'Mean?' she asked cautiously.

'Well . . . first they invade your privacy and harass you; and then when you're all upset they take photographs and make out you were upset about something quite different. Isn't that true?'

'Well yes – you're quite right. That's *exactly* what they did – and it made me so mad!'

'I'm not surprised you're mad – you're quite right to be!' said the quiet voice supportively.

'Are you from some sort of complaints agency?' asked Julia eagerly. Perhaps she could get an apology from those offending newspapers.

'Oh no!' the man gave a friendly laugh. 'No – I'm just a friend of your headmistress and we were talking about you. I was saying – and Mrs Kendall agreed – that you might benefit from some confidential counselling. You know . . . someone to talk to. Someone who would listen to you and help you sort things out. Not many girls have been through what you've been through Julia.'

She nodded silently.

'Apart from anything else, Julia, it must have been quite extraordinary to get to know Hal so well – what a remarkable fellow – I wish I could have met him! And over the weeks I would guess you must have become quite fond of him – and miss him?'

The speaker paused; but only for a moment. 'The reason I phoned was to see if I could be of any use to you. I'd be glad to help.'

'It's very kind of you,' answered Julia and hooking a chair with a foot pulled it to her so that she could settle down to chat in comfort.

It was true – she had no one to talk to about her own feelings: there had been masses of talk about Hal to John, to the professors and men from the Ministry of Defence – she had told them everything she knew; but no one had asked what she *felt* about it all. Her mother seemed to understand in a silent sort of way – but she couldn't explain to her mother (and didn't want to) what she really thought about Hal. One of the problems was she wasn't sure, herself, what she thought or felt. And now she knew Hal was a clone of Ben: did that make him her brother or not? It didn't feel like he was her brother; and yet there was something about him, something familiar and family-like, now she thought about it, which she had always recognised. She had tried talking to Ben but he wasn't much help to her. Once he'd got over the surprise – and shock – at finding that Hal was his twin, he'd taken the cloning to be a sort of compliment to himself. In his own eyes he became the centre of attention and his sister's feelings just didn't enter into it.

She needed to talk with somebody. A girl in her class had once gone to a counsellor when her parents had split up; Julia remembered her saying how helpful he had been. And now here was a sympathetic ear at the end of a telephone; some-one she could tell everything to. It was perfect.

She decided to start at the beginning; about first meeting Hal and finding him so mysterious, foreign but familiar. The man at the other end of the line let her ramble on at her own speed. She had just reached the part of the story where she was telling about sitting at the top of the garden with a newspaper teaching Hal to read, when the back door bell rang.

'Please – just hang on a minute . . . I've got to answer the door. *Please* don't hang up,' she said.

To Julia's great surprise her headmistress stood at the back door. She didn't really want to talk to her just at the moment but then she could hardly send her away.

'Mrs Kendall! How nice to see you . . .' she trailed off.

'Julia! Since you can't come to see us, I thought I'd just pop in to see how you both are! And I'm glad to see you're so well-protected – your policemen wouldn't let me past until I'd shown them my driving licence!'

'What a strange coincidence. There's a friend of yours on the phone just now – he's phoned up to offer me some counselling.'

'A friend of *mine*?' Mrs Kendall looked perplexed. 'What's his name?'

It was Julia's turn to look perplexed as she realised she had never got the man's name.

'Here . . . let me talk to him.'

Julia watched bewildered as her headmistress's face became red with anger. She was even more astonished when she heard her swear down the telephone.

'I'm sorry Julia,' Mrs Kendall said as she replaced the receiver. 'I hope you didn't say too much to that skunk . . . you've been talking to one of the nastiest kind of journalists there is. In fact it was one of the reasons I came to see you. That fellow has been snooping round school for the past few days.'

Life had been completely disrupted for the Garstangs. To Ben and Julia it felt as though it could never return to normal. Weeks passed and they were already half-way through the summer holidays. They should have gone away for a break but somehow it never got organised. Ben ventured out occasionally to windsurf with friends: he was known down on the beach and could spend a whole morning without anyone pointing at him or being harassed by journalists. Sometimes he would notice a lone photographer with a telephoto lens lurking in the distance. He tried to ignore them but the continuous attention, the uneasy feeling of always being watched, was wearing. Most days he stayed at home reading or gazing idly at the TV. Friends sometimes called round to keep him company – particularly Helen.

The glorious garden in Filkins Wood was on Julia's mind all the time; and when she was asleep she dreamed of its beautiful flowers, of the sunbeam tree and the blue curtains of flowering creeper. It was Hal's garden and she longed to go there and explore more of it. If only she could just walk up to the wood and roam amongst the trees she would be happy. But the way was barred. Heavily-armed guards kept everyone out. They stood at the gates to the wood looking like fallen angels in an evil world.

Julia was bored and the way in which she hung around the house, despondently doing nothing, worried her mother. She was nervous about going out anywhere on her own. Julia didn't have a circle of friends in the way Ben did and Betty had long since dropped out of her orbit.

Her days became rather empty and directionless. Dorothy Garstang tried to motivate her daughter by driving her over to the stables and it usually worked for a few hours. But then Julia quickly slid back into silence. Mercifully, she never saw the article that was written about her by the journalist whose name she never did discover. Ben was shown the newspaper by a friend, but he kept quiet about it out of respect for Julia's feelings. STAR-STRUCK JULIA LOSES HER ROMEO, it had been headed. Many things she had never said were attributed to her.

A postcard arrived for Julia one day, however, which put her in a euphoric mood. It had been posted in the far north of Scotland and bore a simple message: 'So much to see and so little time! Longing to tell you all about it. Lots of love. Hal. XX' The postcard arrived at a good time, coinciding with the discovery that the local hedgerows were beginning to heal. Although high summer, buds were appearing on twigs that looked dead; and beneath the same hedges buttercups and fresh green grass brought new life and colour to the scene.

This unexpected spring was not just local.

Familiar flowers began to bloom in unfamiliar places and strange flowers appeared unexpectedly all over the world. By the sea at first, by lakes and rivers, and then further inland, new plants began to grow. They blossomed in nooks and crannies, in open pastures and dense woodland, on mountain-sides and in valleys; everywhere from the remotest regions of Canada to the banks of the Thames where it runs by Kew Gardens.

To the far north of Canada, where ice floes float in the freezing sea it was late in the season of the midnight sun; a pale blue sky faded away into a faint white line along the horizon where distant ranges of mountains were capped with snow. Hunters, Innuit, steered their canoes carefully between the slowly moving sheets of white ice, while grey seals eased themselves into the safety of the sea.

The Innuit, who have twenty different words for the snow in all its various qualities, had no words to describe the extraordinary flowers they found floating between the ice floes. And water lilies were unknown in that region. Smooth cream coloured leaves lay flat on the surface of the water; at the heart of each splay of leaves was a large black bloom. The petals were so dark that they drew the fascinated gaze of the hunters as though down into a hole in the night.

While the astonished Innuit were contemplating the strange newcomer to their seas, thousands of miles away a television camera was pointing at a black tulip in Kew Gardens. The camera focussed on the flower and zoomed in for a close-up.

'. . . and this is just one of the many remarkable blooms that have appeared in Kew Gardens in the past few days . . .' the TV presenter was saying.

It was a perfect specimen. Not the almost-black of many so called black tulips, which have a hint of purple velvet about them, but the much coveted pure black dreamed of by bulb growers for generations. Its neat petals absorbed all colours and reflected no light at all; a miracle of midnight elegance.

'Weird isn't it?' commented Ben to Helen and Julia, who were watching the programme with him. 'Hal is made of the same stuff as all these flowers?'

'I suppose so,' Helen answered. 'But then not so weird really. After all – we're made of the same proteins as the vegetables we eat– that's why we eat them. I know it's not quite the same but still – even that's weird if you think about it too much.'

'Oh, I've had plenty of time to think about things! The only advantage in being stuck here, Helen, is I've been able to watch an awful lot of TV. I tell you, there's not a thing I don't know about DNA, genetic engineering, evolution, astronomy – you name it! The TV companies are going wild cancelling all their regular programmes and giving crash courses in life, the universe, and just about everything!'

'Helen . . . what did *you* think of Hal?' asked Julia.

'I thought he was really nice. But I only talked

with him a couple of times,' she answered and then she added, 'good-looking though!'

'Just like me!' nodded Ben.

Julia ignored his remark.

'Do you think they'll kill him – if they catch him?' She voiced the worry that had been on her mind for a long time, thinking fearfully of Omega-Zed and remembering the note of doubt and mistrust she had detected sometimes in John's voice when they spoke about Hal.

'I suppose they *might* . . .' answered Helen. 'It's quite frightening . . . all that power . . . halting the American navy like that . . . and creating that fog . . . and we've no idea what went down to the sea from Filkins Pool! *And* the snakes! And if they say he's a plant, just part of *Julianum*, then there's nothing to stop them killing him. There's no law about killing plants – unless they're protected species – which he certainly isn't.'

Ben shook his head.

'The law doesn't apply does it? We don't have any laws that deal with Extra Terrestrials.'

They turned their attention back to the screen where the director of the Royal Botanic Gardens at Kew was about to be interviewed. The director of Kew, a shy man, disclaimed all credit for this latest and most remarkable addition to the plant collection of the Royal Botanic Gardens. It was the first time in the history of Kew that a rare species had sown itself in the Gardens and not had to be brought in from elsewhere. The tables had been turned. He had the distinct impression that the place had been chosen quite deliberately. The plants had hunted the Gardens and not the other way round. The director could give no Latin names for most of the flowers viewers were about to see – or even English ones for that matter. Until now *Julianum* had concentrated, mostly, on making copies of known English varieties of plants (the press and TV had not yet been allowed to enter Filkins Woods); but here in Kew it was doing its own thing.

Julianum was showing off splendidly. But to what purpose and why in such a public place?

The cameras began to pan across the flower-beds which had recently erupted from the lawns beneath the trees. Exotic flowers of every shape and hue mixed together in matching shades and tones.

In one direction, bright enamelled colours startled the eye; in another, banks of pastel colours, soft pale blues and gentle pinks swept up from the pathways to tall outlandish blooms in the background. A whole bed of white was set off by the odd red flower. Mysterious purples and indigos glowed in the shade beneath the trees.

Large cream-coloured flowers, that looked as though they had been finely worked from Victorian lace, mingled with slender violet blooms that hung in clusters. Deep red pitcher plants with throats like trombones made a gentle murmur, almost musical, as the breeze blew across them: aeolian pipes of Pan.

A wonderful sense of order made play with rampant disorder; there was nothing artificial or contrived about the way the plants grew together. Everything flourished in wild and beautiful profusion. Butterflies, unrecognisable even to the experts fluttered from bloom to bloom. The camera, following the erratic path of one magenta winged insect swung back to the crowd which had gathered.

Julia suddenly lurched forward to the set and pointed.

'There's Hal! . . . I'm sure it's him . . . look!'

A young man stood at the front of the patient crowd where they had collected behind a rope. As they watched he separated himself from the crowd, stepped over the rope and walked straight towards the camera. He wore a dark well-fitting suit, a white open necked shirt and his blond hair was swept back from his face.

'It *is* him . . . and where did he get that suit from? Doesn't he look great in it?' Julia was on her knees in front of the TV.

'I told him about Oxfam shops,' said Ben, 'and Dad gave him some cash only the day before he left.'

'And he's brushed his hair – just the way you do Ben . . .' Julia was ecstatic to see him.

'I *said* he was handsome . . . and he does look great,' said Helen.

'I bet he fixed all this . . . just to get on TV,' said Ben.

The camera swung away from Hal and the presenter began to speak about the butterflies which had come with the plants but she broke off. The camera returned to Hal. He had been recognised by the programme director. An interview before he was arrested would be the TV scoop of the year.

Hal took complete charge while the presenter stood uneasily at one side.

'I'm Hal. You've seen the picture of my human twin Ben. It's been in all the papers and on many of your newscasts. But don't be taken in by all that you read and hear. You are being fed many false views.

'You have no need to fear anything – except yourselves. You've seen what we can do. But no one has been hurt. We are different from you – and yet we are the same as you. We can live alongside each other . . . there really is nothing to be frightened of – we can easily include you in our plan for the planet.'

'*Include* us? I don't much like the idea of that,' Ben muttered. The others quickly shushed him.

'Don't let yourselves be panicked by ignorant people. Why should we want to destroy the life which has taken three billion years to evolve on your world? We respect life. We *are* life.

Only ignorance leads to destruction. We are the Garden and we are the Knowers of the Garden. We believe in what is beautiful and what is true. Look! See for yourselves!' He gestured around him.

'. . . Do you realise . . . we could save your endangered species? We could prevent your blue whale from becoming extinct – and the humpback; and the bowhead. No plant or creature need disappear into extinction ever again. We will take their DNA into our own being. They will become part of us and live forever. We might even be able to resurrect your dodo from the cells of stuffed museum specimens.

'. . . We can clear up your pollution too: clean up your poisoned rivers and seas: make your world habitable and safe for your children. We can cooperate in peace.

'. . . So what happens next depends on you.'

Two policemen arrived on the scene. They arrested Hal in full view of the cameras and quietly led him away.

If the Innuit, who had discovered the black water lilies, had travelled a thousand miles north of their hunting grounds they would have come across something even more astonishing. The ice fields at the north pole were beginning to swell upwards as though a broad backed gigantic whale was trying to heave its way through to the surface.

Cracks in the arctic ice radiated out from the pole for so many miles that from the air the area began to resemble an enormous dartboard. The true extent of the devastation to the ice fields was revealed on satellite pictures. Many of the fissures in the ice ran for more than a hundred miles from the pole, forming a great star at the axis of the world. The sea surged out of the clefts in the ice and froze in the biting wind.

Scientists at a research station near the pole were quickly airlifted to safety. It was the most unlikely place on earth for a volcano to erupt but that was the only explanation they could immediately offer for the strange phenomenon. A low amount of seismic activity had been recorded though not enough on its own to cause any worries. But then the sea bed had started to move and to rise, displacing prodigious quantities of ocean from beneath the ice. Two submarines, one American and the other Russian, were warned by their respective powers to leave the area quickly, which they did; and only just in time.

Mountain building is a slow process, if it is not volcanic, and normally takes millions of years. Scientists were perplexed. In only seven days a thousand square miles of sea bed had risen up to reach the floating pack ice, swelling like an enormous loaf in an oven.

A new mountain at the northern end of the earth's axis was being born, a mountain which would point straight towards the pole star Polaris.

As the new mountain broke upwards through the white polar landscape, avalanches of ice rumbled and crashed down its slopes. They formed great heaps and screes of glassy fragments; billions of tons of broken iceberg, jumbled at crazy angles, sharp and menacing in the midnight sun.

As fog rolled in hiding the whole fantastic scene, observers realised that this was no ordinary mountain building process. The Garden of Eden seed was manipulating the geology of the earth.

Julianum was doing some landscape gardening.

CHAPTER 17

Omega-Zed

The story of Omega-Zed, when finally leaked to the press, shocked the public. For weeks, people had been mesmerised by the media: no one knew what to think. Did JULIANUM pose a threat? Or was it an exotic and harmless addition to life on earth? Friend or enemy? A plant which grew its own super-intelligent gardener; a plant which could disrupt the geology of the Earth: people wanted to know – should they be *for* it or *against* it?

No one could tell them.

There were no grounds for taking a view either way. Nothing like this had ever happened before.

Now, to make matters worse, there was danger that Omega-Zed, a Doomsday virus, would be released. There were fears that such a virus could never be controlled; and no one knew who was ultimately in charge of it. Speculation and rumour played with people's anxieties.

Meanwhile Omega-Zed was being mass produced in great quantities. Small vials of the lethal virus were flown by airforce jet to the United States, where well-equipped laboratories shared in the dangerous task of manufacturing the organism. When sufficient stocks had been prepared, canisters of the virus were distributed to the armed forces of various countries around the globe. Even traditional enemies were entrusted with the stuff. Disappointed nations, those who were denied access to the biological weapon, raised the matter bitterly in the Council Chamber of the United Nations.

People had often said that the world would only become one united community, one global village, when faced with some common enemy. These prophecies were now being fulfilled. But Omega-Zed had never been used before and no scientists were prepared to predict its long term effects if released into the environment. The awful irony was that the world might well become united as one community only to plan its own suicide.

Surprisingly, no one at an official level asked where Omega-Zed had come from, or how it was that stocks existed, readily at hand, when international germ warfare treaties had banned even the possession of biological weapons. Governments turn blind eyes to almost anything when it suits them.

Professor Duckworth was promised a knight-hood. Tests he had conducted with a mutant version of the original stock of Omega-Zed had proved positive. Flowers of *Julianum* were quickly reduced to a decaying pulp when exposed to infinitesimal quantities of the killer virus. The snakes, too, were one hundred per cent vulnerable to the new strain of Omega-Zed.

Work done in the university laboratory was hailed a success; but John felt sick in the pit of his stomach. It was a love of nature which had led him into biology in the first place. The thought of Omega-Zed sent a shudder down his spine.

'Julia! What a surprise!'

John stepped into the small kitchen of his flat and dumped a carrier bag of fast foods on the top of the fridge.

Julia had her back to him when he walked in. She was at the sink washing up the cups, bowls and plates of the past three days.

'Hi!' Julia answered in a strange whisper, swinging her hair away from her face as she dried her hands on a tea towel. She gave him a kiss.

'I've had a cold and lost my voice,' she explained.

'How did you get in?' he asked.

'The door was unlocked . . . you clot! You're lucky it was me and not a burglar!'

'Well I'm glad for your sake it *was* open –

you might have had to wait a very long time. I didn't know you were coming. You should have phoned.'

'But you never answer . . . you're never in!'

'True,' he nodded. 'I've been at the lab nearly twenty-four hours a day. *Julianum* is ruling our lives.'

'So I've come to look after you for a few days . . . see you eat properly!'

John groaned. 'I suppose that was Mum's idea. But look here, we better phone her . . . let her know you've arrived safely.'

Julia shook her head vigorously. 'No . . . you're far too busy to start worrying about *me*. I can look after myself. Anyway your phone doesn't seem to be working . . . I tried it. I'll pop out later and use that public phone on the corner. OK?'

John readily agreed. He was dreadfully tired. What he really wanted was a bite to eat and a sleep. Julia already had a pan on the stove. He lifted the lid and sniffed – his favourite; vegetable curry.

'I hope you won't get bored,' John said, slumping into a chair. 'I can't take any time off to show you round . . . though we might go to a film tomorrow night.'

'It's OK – I'll entertain myself. It'll be nice to be quiet and to have a break from Ben! He's always arguing these days . . . I'll be all right really . . . I'll read your biochemistry books!'

she whispered hoarsely, casting her eye along his shelf of specialist literature.

'I wish I could show you the labs but without a special pass you'd never get in.'

'Even though my name is Julia?' She looked briefly crestfallen. 'Surely if *Julianum* is named after me I must have *some* rights?'

'Omega-Zed is so dangerous hardly anyone is allowed into the biochemistry labs now. Military guards are everywhere.' He paused. '. . . though I suppose I could take you to the computer buildings . . . security isn't so tight there. We're using computer graphics to build up an idea of Omega-Zed's structure – and *Julianum*'s.'

Julia nodded enthusiastically. 'I'd like that.'

While John was eating (Julia had nibbled enough while preparing the meal) they talked about Hal. There was a rumour that he was to be brought to the university. Blood samples and swabs from his mouth had already been sent for DNA analysis. He had not tried to escape and was, as the papers say, 'cooperating with the authorities'.

'Surely they won't use Omega-Zed on him?' Julia asked searchingly.

'I hope not . . . It wouldn't make sense anyway. We don't know if he's the only one or not – there may be other "space-twins". And we don't know what *Julianum* is going to do next. It clearly has remarkable powers. Better to keep him talking I would think. But *we* don't make the decisions . . . and that's the worst bit of it. I'm feeling really depressed about the whole thing. I've a horrible suspicion that *everything* is going wrong.'

'You're tired. You must get some sleep,' Julia ordered him.

John crashed out on his bed in seconds.

Julia curled up in a sleeping bag, her patched jeans and 'Friends of The Earth' tee-shirt folded neatly on the floor beside her.

During the night a dark blue police prison van, with small barred windows, swept into town. Motor cycles, with lights flashing, preceded and followed it. The van headed for the university and finally came to a halt in the inner quad by the main administration building.

A policeman climbed down from the passenger seat at the front, walked round to the back of the vehicle and by the light of the motor cycle headlights unlocked the rear door.

Two plain clothes officers with a blond young man handcuffed between them climbed carefully down. They marched quickly to the main entrance of the building and were conducted from there to the top floor by an army officer.

Julia asked if she might talk with Hal. She and John spent half an hour with him in a small library at the top of the building where he was being held as an apparently willing prisoner.

Hal seemed older and quieter but in many ways just the same: friendly and genuinely pleased to see them. He apologised for all the fuss he was causing, asked about the family and wanted to hear particularly about Ben. Was he well? What did he think about Hal being his 'Space-twin' as the newspapers called him? Did he mind?

John tried asking questions about the floating islands of water lilies that were appearing in all the oceans and seas of the world: and about the growing mountain Polaris shrouded in fog at the north pole. Hal's eyes took on a glazed distant look – these questions were being put to him all the time. But he laughed when reminded of the U.S.S. *John F. Kennedy*. Hadn't they enjoyed that joke? Then suddenly he became serious as he reflected aloud that human beings seemed to be at the mercy of wild and uncontrolled emotions; anger, fear and pride. Did they not understand themselves? he wondered. It perplexed him to find intelligent creatures so advanced and clever in so many respects, who were motivated and ruled by such primitive feelings.

However much John probed, Hal revealed nothing about his own plans or what *Julianum* was doing world-wide. As for the mountain Polaris, he dismissed the question with a fleeting smile.

The one subject that was not raised at all was Omega-Zed. On the morning of Julia's fifth day of staying with John, she was allowed to visit Hal once more by herself. They spent twenty minutes in quiet conversation until the guard asked her to leave. Three intelligence officers had come to talk with him: the authorities were becoming impatient with the superficial level of 'cooperation' they were receiving from the prisoner.

Julia had spent hours watching the remarkable 3D graphics on screen. There were several strains of Omega-Zed, all of them lethal to life on Earth. Only one had proved successful in killing *Julianum*. Its basic structure was an icosahedron, one of the five perfect solids. Growing from each of its many corners there were complex scaffoldings of molecules. In its own sinister way it was very beautiful.

The researchers knew Omega-Zed was effective. Their task now was to discover its fine structure and so find out why it was so efficient at killing *Julianum* when all else failed. Their other major task was to find a way of controlling and rendering the virus harmless.

Julia delivered a box of sandwiches and asked a guard on duty to hand them on to her brother. She scribbled a short message on a scrap of paper, put it on the table in his flat and left. It was about mid-day.

John was furious when he returned home that evening and found her note: furious with himself. He had meant to take Julia out to a meal and spend a little more time with her. What was worse he felt guilty that he had let her leave without walking her down to the coach station or seeing she had enough cash for the journey. She was too young to be coming and going on her own. He felt irresponsible and angry with her for not telling him when she was leaving.

The phone in his flat had still not been repaired so he walked round to the phone box at the corner straight away.

He got through immediately. His mother answered.

'Hello, Mum! Is Julia home?' he asked.

'Hello dear! Yes she is . . . do you want to speak to her? She's asleep I think. Do you think I could get her to phone you back? I'm sure she'd love to talk to you. But she's not very well. Got a high fever and looking very flushed. I called the doctor out to her but he just said it was some virus or other . . . you know what doctors are these days – don't like to commit themselves.'

'A *virus*?'

A terrible thought swept through John making him grip the phone rather tightly. But then he dismissed it quickly. Omega-Zed worked in seconds.

'Oh . . . I'm sorry . . . poor Julia. I feel rather guilty that I didn't look after her properly.'

'Guilty, dear? . . . what do you mean? Look I'd rather not wake her but I *will* get her to phone you. She'll enjoy that – and it'll be the first time out of her bedroom for three days. She's quite weak poor thing.'

Next morning one main story dominated the head-lines. OMEGA-ZED RELEASED IN SOUTH ATLANTIC.

During the past week, enormous patches of water lilies, each the size of an English county, had spread across the sea at the estuaries of large rivers and near the entrances to the world's principal ports. It was very specific targeting. Although still open, the world's major sea lanes could be closed in a moment. Oil from the Gulf would be cut off; naval powers would be immo-bilised. Everyone knew what *Julianum* had done to the American fleet in the north Atlantic; and everyone was waiting for something to happen. Military leaders became jittery.

It was in this atmosphere of uncertainty and nervous tension that a South American general had ordered the spraying of a carpet of water lilies that looked all set to blockade his country's main port. He disregarded the Agreement 752 of the UN which forbade any single country from using its biological weapon until the Security Council had given the go-ahead.

THE END? Screamed the headlines. DOOMS-DAY VIRUS RELEASED.

A second news item went almost unnoticed. The alien Hal had escaped from custody during the night and his whereabouts were unknown.

215

John had the difficult task of telling Professor Duckworth, his colleagues and the military authorities that for five days *Julianum* had been cooking his supper. He felt such a fool as he broke the news. His own sister! How could he have been so easily deceived? If only he had phoned home earlier as he should have done.

The most worrying thing, from a military point of view, was that the girl had had access to the computers and seen the graphics of Omega-Zed, its molecular structure and its shape.

It was several days before this new development reached the press. The lead story on the front pages continued to be the situation in the South Atlantic. Ships were excluded from the zone; decaying water lilies were surveyed from the safety of the air. Charts of sea currents were scrutinised in detail and calculations made; speed and direction.

Then journalists began to speculate – were there more 'space-twins' around? If *Julianum* had borrowed the genes, the DNA, of Julia for one cloned copy of the girl then why not a dozen? Or a hundred? Or a thousand? And the same for Hal? And who else had had their DNA copied? *Julianum* could be growing its own army.

CHAPTER 18

Yggdrasil

Julia supposed she ought to feel hurt, angry, even jealous perhaps: Hal was now enjoying the company of an exact copy of her. But she felt none of these emotions. At the most she felt frustrated – things were happening all over the world and all she could do was to watch the TV bulletins.

Excitements were passing her by.

Even John had been lucky enough to talk with Hal; for that she did feel envy. But the fact that she too now had a 'space-twin', as the press referred to her clone, only filled her with a sense of pride and pleasure – particularly as it was her twin who had presumably engineered Hal's escape. Everyone around her had become increasingly doubtful about *Julianum's* intentions: it had become a case of 'us and them', or what was even worse, 'us or them'. But Julia herself felt nothing but optimism. She knew in her bones that all would be well in the end, although she had ceased to say so; she got accused of being naive or was shouted down with derision. Even Ben seemed a bit uneasy in his opinion of Hal. Perhaps she had been duped, she wondered to herself sometimes? She had fallen in love with Hal and had eaten from the sunbeam tree. Had eating *Julianum* had an effect upon her? The question was there – but it hardly worried her.

Cameras on board satellites orbiting 150 miles above the ocean kept an eye on the place where the Doomsday Virus had been released. The patch of water lilies covered an area 100 miles by 100 miles. It was spreading, growing in size daily. At the centre, where the plants had been sprayed with Omega-Zed a hole had appeared. It, too, was growing and after three days was over five miles in diameter. It contained a perfectly circular stretch of open sea flat as a mill pond. The surrounding masses of vegetation had a dampening effect on the Atlantic swell and the waves so that the surface was strangely calm.

After five days, when the hole in the carpet of water lilies had expanded to seven miles in diameter, a reconnaissance plane flew low over the area taking close-up pictures and sampling the air.

The atmosphere above the lilies was entirely clear of the virus much to the scientists' relief. But photos revealed immense quantities of decomposing leaves just beneath the surface of the sea. Much of it had sunk beyond view. Dead fish floated everywhere bellies uppermost. It was a stagnant pool of death and decay. The blight was spreading outwards slowly but surely, like a patch of leprosy on the planet. The scar was clearly visible from space: satellite pictures kept TV audiences around the world up-to-date daily.

In the far north, Polaris continued to grow higher, the broad back of the mountain heaving slowly upwards towards the clouds. It was 300 miles across at the base, a rising dome covered in snow and ice, encircled with fog.

In September, the season of the midnight sun came to an end and the Arctic froze in a cold twilight. Only the curved top of the great mountain caught the last rays of the slowly setting sun, a broad snow field raised up into bright daylight above the gathering Arctic night. As the sun sank lower beneath the horizon, so the mountain grew yet higher.

A sharp peak appeared at the high point of the great dome, a pinnacle that thrust its way up towards the stars at an even greater rate. By November it was ten miles high, twice the height of the tallest mountain on earth.

Seismic instruments in the northern hemisphere detected a continuous background 'rumble' from the earth's crust north of Greenland. It was nothing violent or cataclysmic – just an unremitting trace of seismic noise. Geologists were totally mystified by the trillions of tons of rock, which were being shifted daily. No known mechanism, human or geological could move so much matter with such apparent ease and so swiftly. Only the moon, with its daily tidal pull on the oceans of the world, could match the majesty of the process they were now witnessing.

More spires appeared pushing up from the curved back of the broad plateau. Dozens of them, some up to a hundred miles away from the central pinnacle, pointed up into the stratosphere above the clouds and the snow. The long Arctic night gripped the polar regions and the last of the sunlight even left the top of the tallest and central spire of Polaris which by now was approaching an altitude of twenty miles.

Reconnaissance planes returned with photos taken by moonlight of a weird landscape of castle-like towers and peaks, a citadel for titanic giants.

'You can *not* fight a mountain,' drawled an American general with resignation. His Russian counterpart nodded in agreement. A newly formed Combined Command based on the United Nations Peace Keeping Force debated briefly whether Polaris should be bombed. It was quite evidently the focus of *Julianum's* activity. But nuclear bombs would make no more than a dent in its flank: like trying to catch a whale with a bent pin and a piece of string. And there was the nuclear fall-out to consider.

All they could do was watch and wait.

Meanwhile the spreading devastation, caused by Omega-Zed in the South Atlantic, came slowly to a halt when the hole in the carpet of water lilies had reached twelve miles in diameter. After two weeks of apparent inactivity, a sea plane was sent out to land in the stagnant stretch of water. The surface was littered with rotting vegetation and dead fish. Carefully collected samples, taken by men dressed protectively like astronauts, revealed nothing. Not a sign of Omega-Zed anywhere. It had either died out of its own accord or had been destroyed.

The total area of that particular patch of water lilies, had increased enormously – in fact by many times the area lost to Omega-Zed. No one was tempted to deploy the virus again against the flowers. Other islands of lilies continued to flourish at strategic positions in seas and oceans as though poised to strangle ports and shipping lanes. Temporary maps of the floating barrages were faxed to all sea captains so that they could give them a wide berth.

When the peak of Polaris had reached an altitude of twenty miles, geophysicists universally proclaimed that it had reached its maximum height and would grow no more. It had pushed up to its theoretical limit. No mountain on Earth could ever be more than twenty miles high: a simple calculation would show that for anything higher than that, the pressure on the base would be so great it would turn the rocks to liquid and the foundations of the mountain would simply flow away like melted butter.

When Polaris reached thirty miles and then forty the geophysicists scratched their heads and revised their calculations. At fifty miles they made no comment.

The tall pillars and towers of rock which had sprouted up in a ring around the central peak curved inward as they grew until in late November they met and fused with the principal spire. They had become the elegant flying buttresses of a vast cathedral tower. When they had all joined in the stratosphere the mountain began to grow faster.

Infra-red photographs, taken from space, revealed the mountain to be warm. Perhaps liquid rock, magma from the core of the earth, was flowing up inside the flying buttresses? Checks revealed no signs of radiation but an unexpectedly powerful magnetic field was discovered which followed the contours of the mountain. The earth's magnetic field was altered, as a result, as far afield as Siberia and Canada.

By Christmas, Polaris was a hundred miles high, its peak protruding beyond the earth's atmosphere. Earth satellites in polar orbit passed by like low flying aircraft. In photographs taken from space the world looked like a fat apple which was growing a short stalk.

Architects viewed the mountain with professional awe: here was the skyscraper to beat all skyscrapers. It had punched a hole through the sky itself. They speculated about whether it was solid or hollow inside – or honeycombed. If only they could discover the secrets of its structure it would revolutionize the building of cities.

But it was biologists who transformed the world's thinking about Polaris. On Christmas Day an international forum announced its considered view. Polaris was not a mountain at all. It was a tree.

The flying buttresses were an elaborate root system; which explained why the tree was able to grow so much faster after the roots had fused with the main trunk. The biologists likened it to the Indian banyan tree whose roots form a whole jungle of extra trunks around the central bole. They gave the tree an ancient name drawn from mythology – not however the mythology of India but from the pre-Christian tales of the Norse people.

According to Norse mythology a cosmic tree grew at the centre of the world; it was the axis of creation. The World Tree supported the universe and linked Heaven with Earth. It was called Yggdrasil, 'Odin's Horse'. The gigantic tree now growing at the North Pole fitted the part well as it stretched up above the sky.

There were very few eyewitnesses, however, to view the giant tree from close quarters in those winter months. It stood silently in the dark like a ghost against the stars, its mountainous roots soaring upwards in the faint moonlight. Shooting stars fell across the sky in front of the Mountain Tree; and the Northern Lights, velvety curtains of red and green played across the heavens and waved slowly amongst the Tree's newly sprouting branches.

By now Polaris-Yggdrasil was 150 miles high and had stopped growing.

CHAPTER 19

The Butterfly Effect

Julia imagined in a superstitious sort of way, which irritated her but which she could not control, that news would only come from Hal when she stopped expecting it. So long as she went on checking the mat for postcards or asking as soon as she returned home from school if there had been a phone call, there would be no message. The imprisoning rules of the superstition were quite clear.

In the event she was right. When news came it caught her quite unawares.

'Off to the pole then?' asked Ian, a classmate, innocently, as he and Julia collected their books for the first lesson.

Julia's forehead furrowed.

'What?'

'Off to the pole . . .?'

She shook her head.

'I don't know what you mean.'

'You mean you haven't heard?'

'Heard *what*. . .?' She answered rather crossly.

'Well . . . it's in all this morning's papers . . . You and your brother have been invited for discussions – whatever that means – it'll be more a dictation of terms I'd guess – at the foot of Polaris. Sorry – Yggdrasil.'

Julia stopped in her tracks and dropped one of her maths books.

'Why me and Ben? When? No one ever told *us*!'

'Seems the UN were contacted by radio several days ago. Message came from that alien fellow Hal and your space-twin Gaia . . .'

'So *that's* what she calls herself,' Julia interrupted.

'. . . They asked that you two be flown to a safe landing place somewhere this side of the pole . . . they gave the map reference . . . the coordinates you know . . . But the UN wanted to send a delegation of prime ministers and secretaries of state to negotiate. That's why you weren't told I suppose. The news was leaked last night. The UN are still holding out for a summit of World leaders. But they've been told apparently that it's to be a discussion and not a negotiation – and that only you two would do.'

At that moment the headmistress appeared in the corridor.

'Ah . . . Julia! There you are! I'm sorry to interrupt your lessons but could you come with me? Give your books to . . . um . . . Ian isn't it?'

226

Two policemen were waiting in the headmistress's study. Ben was with them already.
They had come, they explained, to take them
home.

During the past few days, as the sun moved
north of the equator, a spectacular sunrise slipped
slowly down the mountainous flanks of Yggdrasil. It was bathed in light from its towering tip
above the ionosphere down to its gigantic rocky
roots. With the passing of the spring equinox the
sun would not set on the titanic tree for the next
six months.

The lower foothills and the roots were the
blue-grey colours of ice and slate. Dark veins
of deep amethyst quartz ran up these pillars of
rock, soaring into the stratosphere way beyond
the highest layers of thin cirrus cloud and
mare's tails of ice crystals. Here and there the
roots were streaked with parallel bands of gold.
Outcrops of rich magenta and ruby warmed in
the sun.

The first branches drooped away from the
main trunk at an altitude of about one hundred
miles. From there on up the Tree developed the
profile of a giant sequoia, the great red wood
tree of California.

The rolls of thick fog that had hidden the
northern Arctic in the very early stages of the
mountain tree's growth had dispersed long ago
– in late autumn in fact. Now, with daylight

227

and clear skies, came the first opportunity for a military expedition to collect rock samples and to drill if possible into one of the roots. If ever the tree was to be conquered with nuclear weapons it would be necessary to know its weak spots.

Meanwhile work was continuing in laboratories on the analysis of *Julianum*. Many of the 'space flowers' in Filkins Wood and in Kew Gardens had produced seeds. At Kew some of the most exotic plants were being successfully propagated and a small committee of horticulturists was formed to give the new plants names.

One great difference was noted; once more an unexpected development. Harry Wolf was the first to draw attention to it.

The cells of second generation 'space flowers' and of the copies they had made of Earth flowers were simple: one nucleus only. The DNA varied from plant to plant. It seemed that, once *Julianum* had adopted a form that it found 'satisfying', it was able to discard all the extra DNA as unnecessary luggage.

Julianum was getting itself even more firmly established on Earth.

Sun glinted off ice as they flew north from Spitzbergen. The landscape was so bright that they had to wear dark glasses which made the powder blue arctic sky look deep azure, almost violet, in colour.

It had been hard at first to persuade their parents. But Julia knew she could trust Hal and would be safe even though she could still hear Harry Wolf's warning words in her ears: 'nice guys aren't always good guys'.

Ben was all for the adventure and voiced the opinion that he would never forgive himself, or anyone else who stopped him, if he didn't go Dorothy Garstang finally agreed when her husband pointed out that they hardly had a choice. The request had come finally from the UN; and Julia and Ben were after all in a very unusual position. They had been chosen, singled out, by circumstances.

John offered to go with them and somehow that seemed to set their mother's mind at rest; though if there *was* danger the presence of John would make precious little difference, Julia thought to herself ruefully.

As the small plane headed north across the icefields towards the Mountain Tree, observers around the world noted a worrying development. The sea-born carpets of water lilies were closing in on ports and harbours; tightening their grip on shipping lanes. The movement appeared deliberate and not merely an accident of the tides. Billions upon billions of tons of fresh floating vegetation were within hours of strangling the waterways of the world. Every major navy would be hamstrung and crippled; international trade brought to a halt.

Julianum seemed to be moving on to the offensive.

A large square table, exactly like the one in the Garstangs' kitchen, and covered in a clean white linen cloth, stood in the snow. A jug of fruit juice was on it, five glasses and a long loaf of bread. A bunch of Lady's Slipper Orchids were arranged in a second jug. Two Przewalski's horses stood patiently in the background: their breath forming small clouds in the brisk air.

It was a strange scene.

Hal greeted Julia with a long hug. Then he embraced Ben and shook hands with John. He introduced them all to Gaia: there was a slight shyness about her as though inside she felt the same way about meeting new people as Julia did. Ben stared at her in astonishment; she was identical to his sister.

There was a formality about the occasion which made them all feel a little awkward – in the way families are when at an anniversary someone is unexpectedly asked to make a speech.

It was Hal who began the serious proceedings. He explained that he was in a dilemma and badly needed their help. The time had come to make a decision: to settle permanently on earth or to leave and search for another world. He had imagined all along that it would be obvious what to do; but now that he came to it he was torn between staying and going.

'But why *us*? . . . how can *we* help you decide?' asked Julia. 'We don't know much about politics . . . or the United Nations . . . or biology . . .'

Hal and Gaia sat at the opposite side of the table, the sun full in their faces. They looked south so that they could keep an eye on the two air force planes parked on the level snow field half a mile away. Sunlight glinted from the zoom lenses of the band of photographers and reporters who had been allowed to travel in the second plane.

Three generals from the Combined Command Force stood apart from the reporters their hands behind their backs. Military personnel beside them kept a vigilant eye on the discussions with powerful binoculars. The two planes and the small crowd of observers were dwarfed by the magnificent landscape: tiny black dots in a vast field of sparkling ice.

Julia and her brothers were dressed for the expected extreme cold. They found to their surprise that the air was relatively mild. Anoraks were unbuttoned, hoods thrown back. The great mass of Polaris-Yggdrasil which reared up into the sky behind Hal and Gaia was generating its own spring climate.

Hal had paused before answering Julia's question: 'Why us?'

'It's hard to explain – the alternatives are peculiarly well-balanced. We need something – a sign, a clue, a hint of some sort to tip us one way or the other. Do we grow the Garden here – or somewhere else? All the time I've been following one path – but now there are two. And they divide *here*. If I take one route I miss all the excitements of the other. And if I take the other – well then I will never know how things would have worked out if I had decided differently!

'*Julianum* has planted itself in many worlds,' he continued. 'There have been difficult worlds and inhospitable worlds, bleak worlds and downright hostile worlds . . .'

'And easy worlds and gentle worlds . . .' Gaia interjected. 'But never one so beautiful and gloriously varied . . . and yet so problematical!'

'Earth has the *ideal* environment for sowing and planting,' Hal continued. 'The perfect soil!'

Julia nodded. She suddenly realised to her surprise that she knew Hal very well. All the talk and all the articles about him being an alien had led her to believe that she only knew him superficially, that basically he was an enigma and quite beyond her understanding. Now she could see that he wasn't a stranger at all. He was as close – even closer – than a brother. She could see too that he was in a real dilemma.

'But that still doesn't answer the question "Why us?"' she said.

Hal paused again before answering. 'We know what everybody else thinks – the politicians, the military people, the commentators and leader writers; that's not the problem. You see we aren't short of information or ideas. We just have to decide. And as the alternatives are so finely balanced we thought it would be fun, and proper, to involve you in the decision. We know you and understand you and love you.'

'On the one hand *Julianum* could colonise the earth,' said Gaia. 'It's a wonderful place. But many of you seem to think it would lead to war – *you* against *us*. That would be no problem for us – an inconvenience but not a problem. It would only be a problem for those foolish enough to begin a war.'

What an irony, thought Julia as she listened to her identical twin across the table. Gaia was still wearing Julia's 'Friends of the Earth' tee-shirt. It was inscribed with the logo: HELP THE EARTH TO FIGHT BACK.

'I decided,' continued Gaia, 'to call myself Gaia because it represented one of the best ideas that has come to mankind in the twentieth century: the idea that Mother Earth is one interlinking living system; that all living things depend upon each other; one self-sustaining and self-regulating web of life wrapped around the world.'

Hal interrupted her with a laugh.

'Not so much philosophy went into the choice of *my* name. I just had to think of something quickly when Ben asked me what I was called. Do you remember that day?'

Ben nodded. 'I wondered why you took so long answering!'

'But many people on earth don't yet know how to live *as* a planet,' continued Julia's twin. They don't know what it is to *be* Gaia. They are still full of self-centredness, one-sidedness, fear, aggression and despair. If we stayed here it might be an uneasy relationship.'

'On the other hand, we could leave,' said Hal. 'We could move on to Venus perhaps; control its suffocating clouds of sulphuric acid and grow The Garden there. Or move further out from the Sun to Titan the great moon of Saturn. It's a cold place, an unguarded wilderness of rock and freezing pools of methane. A challenge!' He paused a moment. 'And so we called you – to help us decide!'

'You can't really expect *us* to tell you what to do surely,' said John.

'No – not in so many words. But what you *say* will help us to see which way the decision falls. And we have already decided that the decision will be made at this table – now.'

'Have you heard of the Butterfly Effect?' asked Gaia.

John nodded but looked puzzled. 'Yes . . . It's a principle by which the effects of some very small event become magnified with time. The flap of a butterfly's wing in the Caribbean can become magnified in its consequences so that it leads to a storm blowing in London. It makes long term weather forecasting impossible for obvious reasons.'

'Exactly so. And it's true in lots of other ways too. The future often hinges on such small apparently insignificant things. Well . . . we're going to ask you a question; and we shall let the Butterfly Effect work in the way you answer it. From your answer, we'll know what to do.'

'The cuckoo,' said Hal. 'Think about the cuckoo.' He paused. 'You know about the cuckoo? . . . about the way it lays its eggs in other birds' nests?'

They nodded.

'Imagine then that you found a small bird's nest and in it, newly laid, a cuckoos' egg.'

A shiver of apprehension ran through Julia and she glanced quickly at her brothers. She remembered suddenly and vividly the premonition she had had almost a year ago. She recalled her tears as she and her brothers walked along the spring hedgerow after the peculiar incident with the orchids. She was sure, quite certain in fact, that she had never referred to this incident, when talking later with Hal. Yet it gave her an eerie feeling to hear him talk of cuckoos' eggs. She had wanted to throw the cuckoo's egg away, to protect the poor hedgesparrow. It had been her brothers who had persuaded her it was better to let things alone and allow the cuckoo to do what was natural and fulfil its aggressive role – whatever the consequences for the weaker bird.

'What would you do?' asked Hal. 'Knowing what the cuckoo will do to its foster brothers and sisters? Would you leave the egg to hatch, the cuckoo to live and make slaves of its foster parents? Or would you, out of kindness to the small bird, take the egg out and throw it away?'

Silence reigned.

A breeze, an upcurrent caused by Polaris-Yggdrasil, stirred the snow in small eddies and died away again.

'I know what we'd do,' said Julia, 'because I know what we did. We'd let the cuckoo have its way. We wouldn't interfere.'

The answer was out. She could have bitten off her tongue. In a few words she had doomed the world to be conquered by the Cuckoo Plant. *Julianum* would rule the earth; and what would happen to people?

The dodo strutted about once more through the last remaining patches of forest in Madagascar. Woolly mammoths roamed the Tundra in northern Siberia. The subdued liquid song of the Dartford Warbler, long absent from its native area, could be heard once more flowing from yellow gorse bushes across the south of England.

In seas and oceans, the water lilies disappeared beneath the waves. They closed their blooms and sank quietly in the night. In a matter of days the oceans were restocked with billions of fish as a river bailiff might restock his stretch of water with a few trout. Seas that had been overfished were filled with multitudes of teeming shoals.

The polluted waters of rivers and seas turned pure overnight.

Prodigious schools of whales, many of the rarer sort, the blue whale, the bowhead and the humpback, spouted playfully far out on the ocean. Millions of acres of plankton and krill satisfied their fresh hunger and the whales sang their songs, ringing their strange melodies through their own watery world.

The earth was a richer place.

Julia's fears had been ill-founded. The choice, which Hal and Gaia made, turned on the idea that one should not interfere with a system which has taken millions of years to evolve. So they decided to leave the Earth and to colonise another world. By restocking the oceans and bringing to life again many of the world's extinct species, the Cuckoo Plant was making a last gift to earth before returning to the sky and its journey through space.

Hal and Gaia could equally well have interpreted Julia's answer differently. They might have decided it meant that the cuckoo's selfish behaviour was to be copied. They could have dominated the earth. But then the Butterfly Effect, in its very essence, is unpredictable.

Soon after their strange meeting at the foot of Polaris-Yggdrasil, the Mountain Tree released its seeds. Instead of falling to earth they were flung in beelines across the heavens and out

237

into the dark night between the stars: ecopods to bring new gardens and new gardeners to new worlds.

When the seeds had been sown into space, two strange craft emerged from the upper branches of the Tree. They circled the Tree-top like pigeons getting their bearings before heading for home; and then they streaked out across the sky high above the blue and unfurled great wings of irridescent colour: giant butterflies in the bright sunlight. The wings fluttered as they adjusted their angles to the sun. Warming in the solar rays they gathered energy, gave a slight correction to the flight of the craft and sailed away from Earth.

Julianum, garden and gardener, was heading out towards Saturn to conquer and control the wilderness on its great moon, Titan, to transform it into a new Eden. Polaris-Yggdrasil stood massive and silent. It had fulfilled its task.

Julia watched the spacecraft go. Would Hal and Gaia change their human forms in order to be able to live in the nitrogen-methane atmosphere of Titan? Would she ever hear from them again?

A selected list of title available from Teens · Mandarin

While every effort is made to keep prices low, it is sometimes necessary to increase prices at short notice. Mandarin Paperbacks reserves the right to show new retail prices on covers which may differ from those previously advertised in the text or elsewhere.

The prices shown below were correct at the time of going to press.

☐	7497 0009 2	**The Secret Diary of Adrian Mole Aged 13¾**	Sue Townsend	£2.50
☐	7497 0101 3	**The Growing Pains of Adrian Mole**	Sue Townsend	£2.50
☐	7497 0018 1	**Behind the Bike Sheds**	Jan Needle	£2.25
☐	416 10352 9	**Lexie**	Mary Hooper	£1.99
☐	416 08282 3	**After Thursday**	Jean Ure	£1.99
☐	416 10192 5	**A Tale of Time City**	Diana Wynne-Jones	£1.99
☐	416 07442 1	**Howl's Moving Castle**	Diana Wynne-Jones	£1.95
☐	416 08822 8	**The Changeover**	Margaret Mahy	£1.95
☐	416 13102 6	**Frankie's Story**	Catherine Sefton	£1.99
☐	416 11962 X	**Teens Book of Love Stories**	Miriam Hodgeson	£1.95
☐	416 12022 9	**Picture Me Falling In Love**	June Foley	£1.99
☐	416 12612 X	**All the Fun of the Fair**	Anthony Masters	£2.25
☐	416 13862 4	**Rough Mix**	Denis Bond	£1.99
☐	416 08082 0	**Teenagers Handbook**	Murphy/Grime	£1.99

All these books are available at your bookshop or newsagent, or can be ordered direct from the publisher. Just tick the titles you want and fill in the form below.

Mandarin Paperbacks, Cash Sales Department, PO Box 11, Falmouth, Cornwall TR10 9EN.

Please send cheque or postal order, no currency, for purchase price quoted and allow the following for postage and packing:

UK	80p for the first book, 20p for each additional book ordered to a maximum charge of £2.00.
BFPO	80p for the first book, 20p for each additional book.
Overseas including Eire	£1.50 for the first book, £1.00 for the second and 30p for each additional book thereafter.

NAME (Block letters) ....

ADDRESS ....

....

....